Praise for The Highlander's Christmas Lassie:

"Swoony Christmas reading. Actually, swoony reading for any time." **Cathryn Hein, bestselling author**

"A beautifully written story filled with emotion, lots of fun and such happiness. It is a heartwarming Christmas story that made me smile with so much joy, oh I do love a good HEA and this one was so good. I do highly recommend this one, I loved it." **5 stars. Romance Book Haven**

"Poignant and moving, this story of reunited lovers will bring the warmth of Christmas spirit to your heart." **Christine Wells, bestselling author of Sisters of the Resistance**

"Malcolm is truly a swoonworthy hero, one very deserving of all the happiness that's bound to come his way. *The Highlander's Christmas Lassie* is an emotional and poignant romance, a warm holiday read with a hero who is the stuff dreams are made of." ***4.5 blue roses. Roses Are Blue Reviews***

"*The Highlander's Christmas Lassie* is the perfect reunion romance for Christmas. Rhona is a strong heroine. Having been left with nothing, she had forged a new life for her and Patrick. Malcolm is a loving hero who never gave up hope or his love. Full of forgiveness, healing and love, *The Highlander's Christmas Lassie* is another wonderful holiday read by Anna Campbell." **Kathy's Review Corner**

"Ms. Campbell's descriptive voice lends itself perfectly to this deeply romantic, passionate story. She weaves the themes of passion, forgiveness, love and hope seamlessly throughout the novel. The characters' conversations are poignant and honest. I loved that a tip from a friend has Malcolm traveling during a snowstorm on Christmas Eve. His determination and faith are a huge part of this superbly written Christmas romance. I highly recommend *The Highlander's Christmas Lassie!* It has all the feels-a devoted hero, heartfelt storyline and a love so strong that will make you believe in Christmas miracles." **Lady Celeste Reads Romance**

"An intensely emotional historical romance from a master storyteller, Anna Campbell's... *The Highlander's Christmas Lassie* is a captivating read rich in passion, emotion and atmosphere...A superb historical novella that tugs at the heartstrings and will bring a tear to the eye, *The Highlander's Christmas Lassie* is an intense and dramatic tale about love lost and found, healing from the past and second chances which held me spellbound from start to finish. Malcolm and Rhona's love story is a mature, emotional and passionate romance readers will fall in love with and find themselves completely and utterly swept away by. Anna Campbell's *The Highlander's Christmas Lassie* is a wonderfully written historical gem romantics everywhere will not want to miss." **Bookish Jottings**

ALSO BY ANNA CAMPBELL

Claiming the Courtesan

Untouched

Tempt the Devil

Captive of Sin

My Reckless Surrender

Midnight's Wild Passion

The Sons of Sin Series:

Seven Nights in a Rogue's Bed

Days of Rakes and Roses

A Rake's Midnight Kiss

What a Duke Dares

A Scoundrel by Moonlight

Three Proposals and a Scandal

The Dashing Widows Series:

The Seduction of Lord Stone

Tempting Mr. Townsend

Winning Lord West

Pursuing Lord Pascal

Charming Sir Charles

Catching Captain Nash

Lord Garson's Bride

The Lairds Most Likely Series:

The Laird's Willful Lass

The Laird's Christmas Kiss

The Highlander's Lost Lady

The Highlander's Defiant Captive

The Highlander's Christmas Quest

The Highlander's English Bride

The Highlander's Forbidden Mistress

The Highlander's Christmas Countess

The Highlander's Rescued Maiden

The Highlander's Christmas Lassie

A Scandal in Mayfair Series:

One Wicked Wish

Two Secret Sins

Three Times Tempted

Christmas Stories:

The Winter Wife

Her Christmas Earl

A Pirate for Christmas

Mistletoe and the Major

A Match Made in Mistletoe

The Christmas Stranger

His Christmas Cinderella (in the anthology A Grosvenor Square Christmas)

Other Books:

These Haunted Hearts

Stranded with the Scottish Earl

The Highlander's Christmas Lassie

The Lairds Most Likely Book 10

ANNA CAMPBELL

To my dear friend Elsa Holland

CHAPTER ONE

Muirburgh, The Trossachs, Scotland, Christmas Eve, 1824

$\mathcal{M}$alcolm Innes, Laird of Dun Carron, turned his weary horse off the Callander Road onto the track leading up to a substantial farmhouse, half-obscured in the thickening snowfall. Hope, high when he arrived in this district, dashed so often since, stirred painfully inside him.

This had to be the place. He'd tried everywhere else in this prosperous little glen near Loch Lomond, before the people at the last house had directed him to Burnside Farm. It was late in the day, and early winter darkness already descended. With an exhausted groan, he dismounted in the empty yard, noticing how well kept the property was.

Senga, his gray mare, was too tired to wander. He led her under the eaves of an outbuilding and rubbed her nose with grateful affection. "I hope this is it for the day, old girl, and we can find ye a nice warm stable out of this weather."

It was madness to travel at this time of year. But when his friend Fergus Mackinnon, Laird of Achnasheen, had told him what he'd seen in Muirburgh, Malcolm couldn't bear to wait for spring and friendlier temperatures. If Fergus was right, almost twenty years of searching came to an end in one way or another today. How appropriate that it was so close to Christmas, the season of miracles and new beginnings.

Senga gave a soft whicker and bumped her noble head into his hand. She was a brave beast with a loyal heart. For her sake, too, he hoped his seeking came to an end.

Leaving her standing, he crossed the snowy yard to the impressive door, decorated with an elaborate wreath of holly and ribbons. He raised the heavy lion-head knocker, and his gut tightened with suspense as the summons echoed inside.

There was a delay before anyone answered. While he waited on the front step, Malcolm pulled down his hat, stamped his feet, and wrapped his arms around himself to warm up.

Or perhaps it only felt like a long wait because he was half-mad with anticipation.

At last he heard a latch lift. The door opened on a lamplit hallway, adorned with branches of pine and holly.

"Good evening, sir."

Malcolm hardly heard the greeting as his heart began to pound. Before him stood a tall youth. A tall youth who wore the same face he saw in the mirror every morning when he shaved.

"By God..." he choked out.

Behind the lad, a slender woman appeared, a mixing bowl in one hand and a wooden spoon in the other. A smiling woman with rich red hair and a face that was a fairer sight than bluebells in an April wood.

A woman Malcolm hadn't seen since he was eighteen years old.

"Who is it, Patrick?" she asked, her voice warm. "Has one of our neighbors called to wish us the best for the season?"

The world receded in a dizzying rush, stealing the strength from Malcolm's legs. To save himself from falling, he reached out a shaking hand to grab the lintel.

"Rhona?" he forced out of a tight throat.

Under his dazed gaze, she stopped in her tracks and went as pale as the snow outside. Her lovely green eyes widened with shock, and her smile evaporated. "Malcolm?"

He gripped the post tighter, in too much turmoil to know exactly what he felt. "They told me ye were dead."

From that moment, the icy hand of despair had descended on him and it had never lifted.

Until now.

He realized that a ray of bright joy pierced the fog of churning emotion inside him. He'd never come to terms with losing Rhona. She'd left a jagged wound in his life that had refused to mend.

To his bewilderment, instead of reacting with happiness or astonishment or curiosity, her porcelain-white face closed against him. He glimpsed a flash of what looked like hatred in her eyes.

"To you, Malcolm Innes, I am dead." Her voice was colder than the wind whistling around his ears. "Shut the door, Patrick. This man isn't welcome in my house."

Before Malcolm could muster a plea or a protest or a question, she turned away and strode off down the long corridor with the proud posture he remembered so well.

Behind her, Rhona Macleod waited for the door to slam shut, but instead she heard her seventeen-year-old son speak. "I think you'd better come in, sir."

"But your mother..."

"I live here, too, and I'd like to talk to you."

Patrick must have noted the resemblance as well. How could he not? With every day that passed, her son looked more and more like his swine of a father. Her son was also more inclined to make peace than seek strife. Patrick had been born one of life's diplomats, a quality he certainly didn't get from his mother.

She faltered in her stride, and for a moment the world around her dissolved into a miasma of crippling distress. Her heart was racing, and she felt sick. She'd never expected to see her first lover's face again this side of the grave.

Once like a pudding-headed fool, she'd dreamed of Malcolm finding her and telling her that everything she believed about him was a lie. But as the years had passed, she'd realized that was never going to happen.

Never say never, Rhona Macleod.

Now he'd turned up, and she wished her former lover to Hades. What a hide he had, bowling up on her doorstep on Christmas Eve without a hint of shame, and expecting a welcome.

Patrick was still talking. "It's as cold as charity out there. Only a villain would force another living creature into such a snowstorm, especially on Christmas Eve."

"I appreciate your kindness. Is there a barn where I can put my horse? She's just about done in."

Bizarre that she still knew Malcolm's voice so well. He sounded almost normal, not stricken as he had when he saw her and made that unconvincing claim that he thought she was dead.

That provided a nice easy excuse to explain his absence, she supposed. She didn't want to believe him, she really didn't. Although not even the hardest heart could miss how distraught he'd looked when he caught sight of her.

As her temper surged anew, Rhona's shoulders stiffened and her sight cleared. She whirled around and glared at her unwanted visitor. "Don't you dare make yourself at home. Go on your way. There's an inn a few miles up the road. They'll fall all over themselves to offer a bed to a fine fellow like the heir to Dun Carron. If you play your cards right, they might even throw in a bonny maidservant to keep you warm."

To her surprise, sardonic amusement creased Malcolm's intense dark face. "Careful, my love. You're starting to sound jealous."

Her queasiness worsened, and bile flooded her mouth with a bitter taste. She felt no urge to smile back. "I was never your love."

The ghost of his humor still hovered. "Of course ye are."

How dare this bastard say that, when they both knew it wasn't true? She bit back the impulse to scream and scratch and carry on like the hysterical girl she'd once been. That was how she'd reacted when brutal men had ripped her away from everything she knew. Her rage had done her no good then. It would do her no good now.

"Betrayal sits oddly with declarations of love. At least in my mind," she said with a dryness that burned. Her hands clutched the bowl and spoon so tightly that she felt the ache up her arms. "But I suppose that's just another sign of what a peasant I am. As if you didn't know that already. Go to the inn, then go back to Dun Carron. Or to hell, for all I care. You have no place here."

"Mother..." Patrick protested, staring at her in dismay.

"This is my house, Patrick," she said in a harsh tone she'd never used to him before. "If you don't like the rules, you can leave."

Rhona turned away again and stomped toward the kitchens. She'd banished Satan from her presence, and she had shortbread to make. But banishing the memory of Malcolm Innes and all that he'd once been to her was nowhere near as simple as refusing the physical man permission to enter her house.

Patrick. His son's name was Patrick. The name rang through Malcolm like a peal of jubilant bells. After all this time, discovering even that much seemed like a victory.

The lad directed an apologetic smile at him. "I'm sorry."

"Don't be. It's no' your fault." Speech was difficult. He still struggled to cope with the magnitude of how everything had changed in the last few minutes.

He had no idea why Rhona was so furious with him. Did she resent his failure to find her? She couldn't have believed the lies his father had told her about Malcolm conniving in their separation.

It was too much for his reeling mind to work through. This morning, he'd been convinced Rhona was dead. Nor had he been sure he'd find his son, despite Fergus's report that in a village near Loch Lomond, there was a youth who was Malcolm's image.

Now he found mother and son. Alive, together, and apparently well. Even the little he'd seen of this farm reeked of prosperity, and both Rhona and Patrick were well-dressed and thriving. Which raised another big question. If Rhona was free and solvent, why the devil hadn't she contacted him?

Eighteen years was a long time. Had she fallen in love with someone else? Did she run this farm with a husband? But even if she did, the girl he knew wouldn't be spiteful enough to keep his son from him.

The acrid thought arose that she might no longer be the girl Malcolm knew.

Except the instant he saw her, his soul had recognized her as the woman he loved. His soul had known that despite their long separation, she remained the Rhona he'd carried in his heart all these years.

Was all that just romantic nonsense?

Romantic nonsense or not, she wasn't chasing him off so easily. "You'd better tell me the way to the inn," Malcolm said with a hint of grimness.

Patrick looked disappointed. "You're leaving?"

"Only for tonight. I'll be back tomorrow. I've hunted ye and your mother for most of my life. A few curt words and a cold shoulder willnae send me away."

Frowning, Patrick glanced out into the yard. With a hunger that felt like a physical ache, Malcolm took the chance to study him. It was a strange experience, meeting an adult child for the first time.

Patrick felt so familiar, at the same time as he felt like a complete stranger. If Rhona had decided she loathed Malcolm, it couldn't have been easy for her to see his likeness every time she looked at her son.

"Mother sent all the farmworkers home for Christmas. You can sleep in the barn, if you don't fancy a ride in the snow. It's warm, and she'll never know."

"I shouldn't say yes. I want to make peace with your mother. Deceiving her isnae the best way to ensure that."

Patrick's smile expressed a flashing charm that Malcolm was sure he'd never possessed. "I'll be blowed if I meet my father at last, only to send him off to perish in a snowdrift."

Malcolm smiled back with an approval that rose from his heart. The lad had courage and a self-confidence that appealed to him. "In that case, show me the barn."

Through Malcolm's roiling confusion, he burned to discover everything about this boy. He prayed that he got the chance. At least his son didn't seem to hate him. As he stared into that thin, dark face, he noted a curiosity that might even match his own.

Patrick grabbed a thick coat from a peg near the door and wrapped it around himself. "Come with me."

It was nearly dark, but there was enough light for Malcolm to catch Senga and lead her into a barn full of quiet, well-fed animals.

Patrick lit a couple of lanterns and gestured to an empty stall. "This will do for your horse."

"Thank you."

"She's a beauty, isn't she?" he said in admiration, as Malcolm settled the mare.

"Ye like horses?"

"I do. But we've got nothing on the farm to match her."

Malcolm bit back a gasp. He felt like someone stuck a knife into his heart. He, too, had been a horse-mad lad. This echo of his younger self in his son made him want to weep.

He needed a few seconds to dislodge the jagged emotion from his throat before he could speak. "The stables at Dun Carron are famous."

Patrick reached out to pat Senga's shoulder. "I'd love to see them."

"You will."

Patrick stared at him, and Malcolm saw the wonder he himself felt reflected in the boy's glowing eyes. "I don't know anything about you. I didn't even know your name, until Mother told you to get out of the house."

That knife in Malcolm's heart twisted, piercing him with a shaft of new agony. What on earth happened here? Did Rhona hate him so much that she couldn't bear to mention his name? That made no sense.

He hoped to God that he had the opportunity to find out what lay behind her hostility. She must know that he'd been a victim of those events eighteen years ago, just as much as she had. They'd destroyed his life. Yet everything indicated that his beloved saw him as more sinner than sinned against.

"I've looked for ye your whole life, Patrick." He spoke slowly and carefully. He didn't want any misunderstandings between him and his son. "Whatever your mother may say about me, I never gave up the hope of meeting you one day."

Patrick regarded him with troubled black eyes. "I've got a lifetime of questions to ask. I feel like I already know you. Yet you're a stranger."

Malcolm smiled at the son he'd longed to find for so long. When he first saw the boy, the resemblance had floored him, but now he started to count differences. Patrick's face was gentler than his, and there was a hint of Rhona's beauty in the arch of his brows and the flare of his nostrils. And something purely himself in the benevolent intelligence shining in the dark eyes. "It's dashed awkward, is it no'?"

Patrick smiled back with a hint of relief, now he heard that Malcolm shared his confusion. "Yes, it is."

Only at that moment did Malcolm recognize something that had tugged at the edges of his awareness since Patrick had opened the door to him. His son had an English accent. The mystery deepened.

Patrick went on. "I want to talk to you for hours. I've got a thousand things I'd love to know. But if I stay out too long tonight, Mother will guess that I didn't send you on your way." He pointed toward a closed door at the end of the aisle running between the stalls. "There's a camp bed in there. I'll try and sneak you out some dinner if I can. I'm sorry I can't offer you warmer hospitality."

Malcolm shook his head, still feeling as if he struggled to keep his balance on shifting sands. "A lifetime of searching has come to an end. That's enough to make this a red-letter day. If I go to bed without any supper, I'll live."

Patrick smiled again. He seemed to be a contented soul. Malcolm could only be grateful. In his darker moments, he'd imagined his son suffering an encyclopedia of horrors without a father to protect him.

"Mother will come round."

Given his earlier reception and Malcolm's memory of the younger Rhona's stubbornness, he wasn't so sure about that, but he admired Patrick's optimism. He clapped him on the shoulder, all too aware that this was the first time he'd ever touched his almost-grown son. The urge to hug the boy close was nigh on overwhelming, but he didn't yet have that right.

By God, he'd have the right before next Christmas, whatever Rhona thought about the matter.

"You'd better go," he said gruffly. "We'll talk tomorrow, even if we have to do it at the inn."

"Yes, we will." Patrick sent him a searching look that made him look older than his seventeen years. He held out a steady hand. "I'm very pleased to meet you, Father."

When Malcolm grasped Patrick's hand, a stinging mist obscured his vision. He had to blink and clear his throat again before he spoke. "Aye, son, it's splendid to meet you, too."

CHAPTER TWO

"My softhearted son has been at it again," a toneless feminine voice said from the entrance to the stall. "Softhearted, not to mention softheaded."

Now Malcolm had accepted that Rhona was alive, her presence shouldn't punch him in the belly with that same visceral impact. But the sound of her voice still made his heart leap high to lodge in his throat.

Perhaps his memory played tricks, but it was lower and huskier than the voice that had haunted his dreams. No trace of her Scottish accent remained.

"Rhona..." He looked up from where he groomed a fine bay colt. He'd rubbed Senga down and given her oats and water, then decided to see what he could do for the other half dozen horses in the barn.

"Don't bother pretending that Patrick didn't ask you to stay." She wore a thick coat, and her head was wrapped in a plaid shawl. At her side, she carried a lidded basket.

"Dinnae take it out on him." He tried a placatory smile. It was a waste of time. She didn't smile back. "He was worried about me making it through the snow."

Fine green eyes flashed with outrage. "Don't you dare to presume to explain my son's behavior to me. Five minutes in his company doesn't offer you any special insight."

With a pang, Malcolm noticed the way she emphasized the "my" in "my son." He already knew he had a long way to go with her before she accepted that he had any role in her life or Patrick's. She was even further from viewing him as a welcome presence.

Sighing and wondering how he could be both so elated and so despairing at the same time, Malcolm set the currycomb on a shelf. The bay whickered uneasily and shifted from hoof to hoof, as it sensed the troubled currents flowing between the two humans.

Malcolm stepped away from the colt and closer to the woman he'd last seen eighteen years ago. He kept his voice even and soothing, the way he'd talk to a skittish horse. "I have nae intention of driving a wedge between you and Patrick."

Dislike hardened her gaze, but even after all this time, he knew her well enough to perceive the apprehension lurking beneath her bristling hostility. "You couldn't do that if you tried."

He spread his hands in a gesture that he hoped indicated he meant peace. "Rhona, I'm really no' here to cause trouble. Trust me."

Her growl told him what she thought of that suggestion. He cursed himself. Trust was the wrong thing to mention, although he still didn't know what he'd done to earn such implacable hatred.

Once she'd adored him, just as he'd adored her. He reminded himself that was half a lifetime ago.

"Too late for that," she snapped.

A grief so powerful that it verged on agony flooded him. Too late to see Patrick grow up. Too late to share nearly twenty years of troubles and joys with the woman he loved. Perhaps even too late to salvage anything at all from the catastrophe of so long ago.

But by heaven, he had to try. The first thing he needed to do was convince Rhona he wasn't some monster poised to destroy her life, even if tonight wasn't the best time to get her to listen to him.

For most of his adult life, he'd survived on the frailest strand of hope. Surely after today, he could cling to hope a little longer. Against all the odds, he'd found his son. Even more miraculous, he'd found his lost love alive and prospering. Compared to where he'd been this morning, he had cause for optimism, even if Rhona was glowering at him the way she'd glower at an adder slithering across her path.

"Are ye here to tell me to go to the inn?" Devil take it, he was reluctant to go. After all the lonely years, some superstitious fear insisted that now he'd found her, he must never leave her again. Or else she might disappear from his life the way she had before. But this time, he'd never find her again, no matter how hard he searched. "If you are, I'll go, but it's a reprieve no' a rescue. I'll be back tomorrow. You willnae chase me off so easily."

That cold gaze didn't soften. "Better you go back to Dun Carron. There's nothing for you here."

How wrong she was. This isolated farm held his entire world. He'd felt half-dead during these years without her. Even with Rhona hating him, he felt more alive at this moment than he had at any time since they'd parted.

Be careful, Malcolm. You know nothing of her circumstances. Don't start building castles in the air.

It was too late. As a boy, he'd given her his heart. That heart was still hers, despite time and separation and sorrow. That heart wouldn't relinquish the hope of her until it stopped beating altogether.

Malcolm said none of this, because even the world's stupidest man could see that she was a million miles away from being ready to hear it. Perhaps she'd never be ready to hear it. But he had to try to establish a truce, and be damned if he was going to let her seething resentment banish him before he had a chance to know his son.

"Now I've found you, I'm no' giving up."

Her eyes narrowed on him as if he was her enemy. "I'll show you the door."

"You may have forgotten, Rhona, but I'm a patient man and a determined one." Regret stabbed him, along with more puzzlement. "A pout and a sulky look willnae frighten me off when I want something."

He saw her fear bubble closer to the surface. "You won't take Patrick away from me."

Dear God. He was horrified that she could imagine he meant her any harm. He made another calming gesture and kept his voice steady. "Don't be a henwit, lassie. I dinnae want to take him away from you, but he has a right to ken his father."

"I'll fight you."

He heaved another sigh, heavier this time. "Ye don't have to." He gentled his voice. "This has been a shock. For the three of us. You're in nae frame of mind to listen to me right now, so I'll go. But I'll come back tomorrow, after we've all had a chance to reflect on what's happened. You and I can talk then."

"You might have made it to the inn an hour ago. You wouldn't get five yards now." Displeasure flattened her lips. "I'm not going to spend Christmas Day digging your stiff and frozen corpse out of a snowy ditch. You've caused me enough trouble already."

He gave a grunt of admiring laughter. She wasn't going to make this easy for him. She'd been a termagant as a girl when her temper flared. She still burned bright as a beacon. If he'd ever feared that life had defeated fiery Rhona Macleod, he knew better now. He was thankful for that, even if he wished she hadn't chosen him as her target. "And I intend to cause ye more."

"Tell me something I don't know."

"Thank you for offering me your hospitality." He ignored the disdainful arch of her eyebrows, although they both knew that calling her grudging cooperation hospitality was an exaggeration.

Her sigh indicated endless annoyance, then her eyes sharpened on him. "What on earth are you doing, playing the stablehand?"

He leaned against the side of the stall. The way she vibrated with hostility told him to keep his distance. "I had a lot to think about. I couldn't settle down, so I decided to be useful."

After meeting his son and discovering Rhona was alive, his head and heart had been in a ferment. Despite his exhaustion, he was too keyed up to sit still. He felt like he must burst out of his skin, unless he found some way to use up his energy. Not to mention that hard work helped him to ignore his rumbling stomach. He hadn't eaten since breakfast.

Rhona stepped back and waved toward two hay bales in the aisle. "I might have rocks in my head, but I brought you some supper." She must have seen his surprise, because she continued in a stony tone. "It's no gesture of reconciliation, so don't imagine it is."

"I wouldnae presume," he said, echoing her earlier accusation.

Still looking like she might explode at any moment, she waited for him to sit down, then passed him the basket. He'd been too focused on Rhona and the emotions raging between them to notice that it emitted a delicious aroma. When he lifted the lid, he found a bowl of rich beef stew, a couple of slices of buttered bread, and a flask that he guessed contained ale. "This is a braw feast indeed. Thank you."

"Eat it before it gets cold."

Malcolm took the ungracious invitation at face value. He spread the white napkin over his knee, lifted the plate and a fork and began to eat. "This is good."

It was. It would have been even better if she'd invited him to eat at a table inside the house, instead of in the barn. But something in Rhona's flinty manner told him that the barn was as close as she meant to let him get to her tonight.

He should be grateful that she offered him even that much. Right now, he could be a couple of miles away at the inn, having battled his way there through a snowstorm.

After a little while, she unbuttoned her coat and perched on the bale opposite him to watch him eat. Her forbidding expression didn't encourage questions. Since they'd come so close to quarrelling, she'd banked her hostility, but it still simmered close to the surface.

Nonetheless Malcolm wasn't altogether dissatisfied with the way things were going. He was still here. She'd deigned to feed him. However much, however inexplicably, she might hate him, he was in a better place than he'd been in two hours ago.

She slid the shawl away from her head. In the golden lamplight, her extraordinary beauty pierced him like an arrow. Under the heavy coat, she was dressed in a high-collared plaid dress in reds and blues. With her vibrant hair and pale skin, she'd always favored vivid colours. That hadn't changed either, he was pleased to note. She'd been a breathtakingly pretty girl, but the years had refined that prettiness to a pure delicacy that enthralled him.

He'd spent years dreaming of her and mourning her loss. It seemed unbelievable that she was here with him tonight. To all appearances, whole and unharmed.

Ignoring her glare, he took the time to study the changes in her. Her face had thinned, and her high, slanted cheekbones lent her features a tinge of the exotic. Fine, winged eyebrows, darker than her hair, arched over large eyes of a peridot green he'd never seen on anyone else. A straight, rather haughty nose. A pointed chin. A pink mouth that had once been soft and full and passionate. Now that mouth was stern and unsmiling.

She'd been a sparkling girl. Her vivacity was one of the things that made him fall in love with her. This austere, spectacular woman who stared back at him as if she loathed him didn't sparkle. Instead she had the icy glitter of a perfect diamond.

Malcolm could already see that maturity lent her a strength that had only been a promise in her younger self. He burned to discover what had made her into the woman she was today. Curiosity ate at him like acid, but he reminded himself to be patient. In time, he'd find everything out.

He was using the bread to mop up the last of the gravy when she spoke again, her voice uncompromising. "What do you want, Malcolm?"

He looked up with a frown. "I wanted to find my son."

"Why?" The question was as deadly as a bullet.

Baffled, he frowned. "Because he's my son."

"That's a surprise. You weren't so eager to claim him when I told you I was pregnant."

Every word she spoke made less sense than the last. "What do ye mean? I asked you to marry me."

"Then you set your father and a pack of the castle's brawniest servants on me, with an offer to pay me to go away. Your father was adamant that Dun Carron's heir could look higher for his lady than a slut of a crofter's daughter. A slut who already carried a bastard in her belly." Old bitterness weighted her voice.

Malcolm winced, even as he recognized the tone. Since he'd lost her, he'd lived with bitterness every second. It had a habit of souring and distorting even the slightest hint of good. "You cannae believe that I had anything to do with that," he said, appalled.

He knew what had happened to Rhona that day. His father had been proud of what he'd done. He hadn't hesitated to crow to his son about how he'd banished the presumptuous tart with ambitions to marry above herself.

Malcolm found Rhona's dismissive shrug unconvincing. "You weren't there to offer any argument otherwise."

With shaking hands, he set his empty bowl aside. He'd enjoyed his dinner, but now the hearty food formed a rancid, uncomfortable lump in his stomach. "I wasnae there, because my father had chained me in the dungeons."

A silence crashed down. Her mouth dropped open with astonishment. Then doubt shadowed her remarkable eyes. "That doesn't sound likely. It's the nineteenth century, not the twelfth. And your parents doted on you. If they hadn't held such high hopes for you, they wouldn't have been so furious that you'd sullied the Innes lineage by consorting with a humble creature like Rhona Macleod."

"Nevertheless, it's true." His voice was hard. As hard as hers. Ridiculous so long afterward to feel stinging hurt, but hurt he felt. Although if Rhona had believed in his perfidy all these years, it explained her anger. "But even more shocking to me is that after everything we were to each other, after all the promises we made, you'd believe that I'd wrong ye like that."

"Young men tell pretty lies to make stupid girls lie down with them." More of that bitterness that sliced at his soul.

She'd once been so bright and joyful. It pained him to see how the years had scarred her. Although what else could he expect? Especially if she believed, as it was so obvious she did, that the man who took her virginity had deceived her.

"You weren't a stupid girl." He'd always delighted in her cleverness.

Her lips turned down. What he'd give for her to smile at him as she once had, as though he was her whole world and she found that world a complete delight. But those sweet days were gone, never to be reclaimed.

"The evidence would suggest otherwise."

"Actually I'll rephrase that. You were a stupid girl to believe that I'd turned my back on ye. You knew I loved you."

The mention of love made her flinch. "At least that's what you said."

He regarded her steadily, willing her to remember the strength of the bond between them. "You didnae trust it was true?"

"Your father was scathing about my chances of becoming his daughter-in-law, and my father was sober enough that night to be furious and humiliated. He wasn't pleased to hear that his daughter was with child and no wedding ring on her finger." She spoke in a heated rush. "And there was not one peep from you to say that they were wrong."

Jimmy Macleod had still been angry when Malcolm tracked him down, drinking himself into oblivion in Aberdeen. It turned out that Malcolm's father had offered the man money as well. In return, Jimmy had to leave the Dun Carron estate and never return.

"So ye took the money and left without a fight?" He couldn't help being disappointed. They might have both lost, but at least he'd gone down fighting.

He should have known better than to doubt her.

Her glance was contemptuous. "As if I would. At that stage, I still thought you were Sir Galahad and you'd come galloping over the hill to my rescue."

If only he'd been able to. He'd raged, he'd sworn, he'd even damn well wept, but nothing had persuaded his father to unlock the chains. Chains that as far as he knew had last been used when the English penned a dozen Jacobite rebels in the dungeons after the '45 Rebellion.

And all the time he'd been aware that despite his good intentions, he was the one at fault. He was responsible for this disaster. Malcolm had been so catastrophically stupid. So trusting. So sure that the whole world would view his love with kindness.

He'd gone straight from learning that Rhona expected his child to telling his parents he intended to marry her. His parents had taken the news that their only son was about to wed a penniless nobody with what he'd soon realized was suspicious composure. Later that night, a gang of servants had rousted him from his bed and shackled him in the dungeons. He guessed they were the same men who had descended on the Macleod croft with his father to bully Rhona.

His parents had always indulged him, so it never occurred to him that they'd resist his will in this, the one thing in his life he really wanted. It should have. Both his mother and father were implacable in insisting that marriage to Rhona would ruin his future.

While he was trapped in the depths of Dun Carron Castle, the father he'd always loved was making sure that Malcolm's unsuitable sweetheart disappeared from the glen forever. Malcolm still hated to think back to those long hours of incarceration, as disbelief and anger gradually turned to soul-devouring despair. He still woke shaking and sweating from nightmares about it. Nightmares where he was back in that dungeon, helpless to stop his life from shriveling into a desolate wilderness.

By the time his father let him go three days later, Malcolm already knew it was too late. Which didn't stop him from rushing to the Macleod croft to find Rhona. But the tumbledown cottage was empty, with no hint left behind of where its inhabitants had gone.

"I let ye down," he said grimly. "No' on purpose, but we should have run off together before anyone could come between us."

She observed him with a troubled gaze. At least she didn't look like she loathed him anymore. Mention of the dungeon seemed to have earned him a scrap of leniency. Was she starting to believe his story?

"We were young. I was just seventeen. You were just eighteen. Perhaps your parents were right, and we were too young to think about marriage."

He hadn't been too young. He'd always known that the only girl he'd ever love was Rhona Macleod, with her passionate soul and vivid red hair.

"It wasnae just about us. We'd made a baby."

For one fleeting instant, she looked devastated. Then she made a dejected gesture. "It was all so long ago."

He frowned at her. "Have ye forgotten?"

She stared down into her lap, her shoulders taut as if she, too, relived those harrowing days. His mouth tasted rank with the defeat he'd suffered in that dungeon, and he could still feel the cold, rough weight of phantom chains.

"No," she said in a low voice. "No, I've never forgotten."

"Neither have I."

When she glanced up, the gaze she leveled on him was questioning but not hostile. She looked vulnerable and much younger. She could almost be the girl he'd loved so long ago. "Did you eventually accept that I'd gone and it was time to get on with your life?"

He responded with another unamused grunt of laughter. "Hell, no. My father kept me in prison for three days and the minute I was free, I headed out to look for ye, but nobody on the estate was talking. I didn't give up. Over the months, I searched for miles around, all the way to Aberdeen. I found your father there, but he said he didn't ken where they'd taken you. Finally, I managed to bribe one of the castle servants to tell me what they'd done. I suppose by then, the fellow thought I had nae hope of finding you, so there was little danger confessing all."

"Because I was in London."

"My father must have been bloody terrified, if he sent ye all the way to England."

She sighed and regret weighted her gaze. It seemed she was ready to believe him at last. What stung like nettles was that she had ever doubted him. He'd never doubted her. "Your father made it very clear that I was no longer welcome anywhere near Dun Carron. Or Dun Carron's heir. What he also made clear was that he acted at your behest."

Grief made his belly clench. Grief, remorse, and guilt. "I'm sorry that I didn't do enough to make ye trust me. I thought I had. I trusted you. When I was with you, I felt invincible. Our love was so strong, nothing could defeat it."

Her expression was bleak. "Yet a determined parent and half a dozen stalwart servants brought us to ruin." She paused. "I should have at least absolved you of conspiring to exile me. Everything I knew of you said that you'd give me my marching orders in person."

She definitely no longer sounded like she hated him. Instead she sounded tired and sad. Malcolm wasn't sure it was much of an improvement. He answered her with the truth that had lived in his heart for most of his life. "I would never give ye your marching orders. You were the reason behind my every breath."

She still was.

Rhona went back to looking troubled. "You're right. We should have run away."

"Even if my father disowned me, we'd have been together. Patrick would have grown up, knowing that his father loved him."

Malcolm had a vision of what these last barren years might have been like if he and Rhona had married. Then from long habit, he shut down the pictures filling his mind. When he'd first started searching for her, convinced that fate couldn't be cruel enough to keep such true lovers apart, his fantasies about making a life with Rhona and his as-yet unborn child had spurred his efforts. But as weeks turned into months turned into lonely years, those hopes had become too painful to revisit.

Now, sitting with Rhona, having met the exceptional young man they'd created together, the thought of everything he'd missed was excruciating. He could hardly bear that Rhona had spent all these years convinced of his betrayal. If they ended tonight with her acknowledging that he'd never forsaken her, never given up searching, it would be some consolation.

Malcolm forced himself back to his tale. "So I went to London and did my best to trace ye. I tried all the inns. I checked the passenger lists of every boat that had left the port since you'd gone. I put notices in papers up and down the country, asking for news of Rhona Macleod and offering a reward for information. That ended up being a mistake. I and the people I'd hired to help me spent too much time tracing false leads. And all the time, nae real information emerged. I started to feel like I chased a ghost. I traveled to Europe. I ended up spending a year in America."

He'd checked the brothels everywhere he went, too. The idea that Rhona might have ended up selling herself had been torture.

Wondering, she looked at him. Astonishment wiped out her earlier doubt. "You did all that? For me?"

"I would have done more," he said, his tone grim. "Until five years into my search, I received a letter from your father saying that you'd died in Ireland. He didnae mention the baby."

"But I was never in Ireland."

"Which makes sense because my agents and I combed every inch of the place, finding nae trace of you." Malcolm's lips twisted in a grimace. "Once I got the letter, I went straightaway to Dundee, where your father was when he wrote, but he was long gone and I never heard from him again."

Old rancor sharpened her reply. "He's always been good at disappearing. He disappeared often enough at Dun Carron when he was on a spree."

"I discovered after my father's death that he'd continued to pay your father an allowance to stay away." Pity thickened his tone. "I'm sorry, Rhona, but I think your father has passed away. The papers I found at Dun Carron indicated that the allowance stopped a year after the letter from Dundee."

She sighed and made a hopeless gesture. Longstanding sadness marked her features. "Any allowance he received would have gone in whisky. He never recovered from Ma's death. I don't think he cared one way or the other whether he lived or died. He certainly never cared much for me, even before your father bribed him to turn a blind eye to what happened."

Jimmy Macleod's intemperate habits hadn't helped Malcolm's case, when he told his parents he wanted to marry Rhona. "Ye deserved better."

Her lips tightened. "I'm starting to think we both did."

"I suspect now that my father paid your father to write the letter saying ye were dead, so that I abandoned my quest. He wanted me to take up my duties at Dun Carron."

"You should have."

He shook his head. "No, there was a chance the baby had survived. If I couldn't have you, I could still have my bairn."

"Oh, Malcolm..." Her eyes were dark with regret and pity. "I shouldn't have raged at you all these years. But everything that happened fitted in with my fears. I could never quite believe I was good enough for the heir to Dun Carron. Your father was right about that. You were rich and fine and handsome and highborn. I was an ignorant hoyden of a crofter's daughter. What could I offer such a paragon as Malcolm Innes?"

For the first time, he managed a genuine smile. "You're the most beautiful girl I've ever seen. You're smart and funny and brave, and you've held my heart since I was old enough to give it. There's nobody to rival ye, Rhona."

She didn't seem to notice his use of the present tense.

When she shook her head, her expression relaxed a fraction. "That's not how I remember it." The faint ease seeped from her features. "So when the laird was so insistent that you'd sent him to do your dirty work, something in me was feeble enough to believe it. At first, he just offered me money to disappear. But I refused to go. Things only got rough after that."

Outraged, Malcolm surged toward her, but she waved him back. "Oh, nothing too bad. I wasn't injured, at least. They tied me up and bundled me into a carriage and took me away."

Her explanation did nothing to allay his dismay. He loathed to think of her sufferings. "You must have been terrified. I cannae believe my father was so ruthless. I'd always considered him a man of honor."

"He acted according to his lights. You were his heir and only child. I wasn't part of his plan at all."

"That's very tolerant of ye," he said, sure that she didn't really feel like that.

"I've had plenty of time to think about what happened." Her tone was resigned. "At least he didn't kill me. I feared he might at first."

Malcolm couldn't bear to imagine what she must have thought when violent men ripped her away from everything she knew and loved. A young girl, alone, afraid, defenseless, and carrying her lover's child. The thought set nausea seething in his gut.

"Dumping ye alone in London to fend for yourself could have been a death sentence." Her pregnancy would put respectable work out of reach.

She must have read his thoughts, because she made a dismissive gesture. "I never had to sell myself. I found kindness where I was most likely to come to grief."

Malcolm should be relieved, but he wasn't sure he believed her. "Rhona..."

"I'm not saying that just to salve your conscience." Even after all this time, she could still read his reactions. "I prospered in the city. You don't have to imagine me servicing a string of men to keep body and soul together."

He took a breath to fill starved lungs and banished the hideous images that had pursued him since he'd lost her. "I worried about that for years and blamed myself."

She shook her head. "I'm quite respectable. Well, almost."

He cut the air with one hand. "Do ye think I'd despise you if you'd taken that path? Even if you'd swived every man in the King's Navy, I could never despise you. I'm just so bloody grateful that you stayed alive. You cannae imagine how I felt when I heard you were dead."

The news had sent him spiraling into a dark pit of hopelessness and misery. He'd wanted to die himself. For a long time, life had lost all purpose, until he decided to gamble on the chance that his child might be alive.

More of that compassion deepened her eyes. "I'm sorry. Once things had settled down, I could have written to you, I suppose, and let you know that all was well."

He tried to see things from her point of view. "You were convinced I'd abandoned ye with a callous disregard for your welfare and feelings."

"Yes." She paused. "What can all this ancient history matter? I suppose you married and had children. You owed it to your name after all."

He sent her a straight look. "I vowed to my father that if I couldnae marry you, I wouldn't marry anybody."

Incredulity widened her eyes. "But when we parted, you weren't much more than a boy."

"Perhaps. I still knew my mind." He drew in a shuddering breath and gave her the stark truth. "I kept that vow. I've never married. I've been alone all my life, Rhona. I have nae children but the one we made together. The estate is mine to dispose of as I wish, so I want to make Patrick my heir."

CHAPTER THREE

Rhona stared in shock at this man who in any reasonable world should be a stranger, but who didn't feel like a stranger. In her memory, Malcolm Innes had remained the gloriously handsome and lighthearted boy she'd loved with such reckless abandon. But this man before her had an intimate acquaintance with suffering.

He was still handsome. Age could never mar that perfect bone structure. The high cheekbones and straight nose and defined, angular jaw remained the same. But the thick, satiny hair was no longer pure ebony. Instead, it was streaked with silver, although at thirty-six, he was in the prime of life. And nobody who looked into those intense dark eyes would imagine that this was a happy man.

Her gloved hands fisted against the hay bale she sat upon. She'd spent years hating him, the other side of the coin from loving him so completely. Before their tragic separation, he'd been everything to her. She'd spent so much time sure she'd been wrong to give her trust and her heart to Malcolm Innes.

Now it turned out his travails had been far worse than hers. His travails still continued. She'd found purpose and a place in the world. More, she'd had Patrick to love and tend and guide. Her son had given her a reason for living. Malcolm had had nothing but an empty life and an increasingly hopeless search for a child who he must fear was dead.

When she thought of her girlhood lover, and despite her anger, she'd often thought of him, she'd whipped up her self-righteous indignation by imagining he never gave her or his son a second's consideration. She'd pictured him marrying some horse-faced, blue-blooded harridan who made his life a misery and presented him with a brood of horse-faced children.

When she really wanted to torment herself, that unknown blue-blooded lady was bonny and charming, and Malcolm's lying eyes looked at her just as he'd once looked at Rhona. Then her mind had also summoned up children who were beautiful and bright, and happy to bask in their father's love. A father's love her own dear Patrick would never know.

Now as she studied this man worn down by long years of sorrow, she wanted to cry. She wanted to take back every curse she'd ever laid on her first lover's dark head. With a desperation that futility couldn't seem to temper, she wanted to make everything better, to heal the wounds that festered inside him.

As the silence extended, his sardonic humor reappeared. "Say something, Rhona."

She swallowed to shift the painful lump of emotion blocking her throat. "I can't believe you've found no comfort or connection in all this time."

He shrugged as if the matter was insignificant. "Whether you believe it or no', it's true."

"But your parents must have done their best to make you marry."

His snort was scornful. "Aye, they did. Until my father died, a bitter man, six years ago, they must have paraded every suitable girl in the Highlands before me. My mother is still alive. She has a house in Edinburgh. At last, she's given up trying to interest me in marriage. I think she's come to regret tearing the two of us apart, although she'd never admit it. She'll love Patrick when she meets him."

Until her brutal banishment, Rhona had liked and admired Malcolm's mother. Everyone in the glen had. The Lady of Dun Carron had been closely concerned in the clan's welfare.

Malcolm's father had been a good and fair laird, too. No wonder his reaction had taken Malcolm and Rhona by surprise, although looking back, she also recalled the laird's oft-stated pride in his Innes bloodlines. When he'd sent her away, he'd been frank about not allowing a lowly Macleod to pollute the family escutcheon. She still cringed to recall his unconcealed disdain for her pretensions to marry the heir.

"You should have settled down with one of those girls," she said. "I can't bear to think that you've found no joy or affection in all this time."

Although looking at him, impossible as it seemed, she could reach no other conclusion. He was thin and wary and ready to bare his teeth at a kind gesture. He reminded her of a starving wolf.

Perhaps she should be afraid. After all, wolves could kill. But all she could think was how heartbreakingly lonely Malcolm's life had been.

Yet despite how close he looked to the limits of endurance, he was still beautiful. Anguish had pared him down to his essence and left him powerful and true.

Bleak black eyes shot her a burning glance. When she'd known him, those eyes had shone with laughter and sheer pleasure in living. She knew now that he hadn't experienced either of those things in close to two decades.

"How could I marry someone else?" His voice was different, too. Deeper and with a somber note foreign to her ardent suitor. "I'd known love, real love. I couldnae accept its counterfeit."

She shifted in discomfort, hearing the hay rustle beneath her. After what he'd just told her, she was painfully aware that she'd wronged him by not believing in him, despite persuasive evidence that he'd deceived her. He'd kept faith. He'd kept faith, even when every sign had pointed to both Rhona and her son dying.

She struggled to imagine how he must feel, now he'd discovered that not only his child but his first love had survived. Not just survived but thrived.

Learning that he'd never given up on her left her reeling, not sure how she should react. One hand made a helpless gesture. "I feel..."

His lips turned down in what she came to realize counted as a smile in his world. "Overwhelmed?"

She ventured a shaky smile back. "Flabbergasted. Like a giant hand has picked me up from the everyday world I know so well and plopped me down in the middle of a magical new land. It's all too much to comprehend, let alone for me to summon any coherent response."

His gaze softened and for a fleeting moment, she glimpsed the ghost of her Malcolm. And that ghost was damnably alluring. For years, seething resentment had stolen her first love from her. What she believed to be his perfidy had turned everything they'd shared into a lie. Whatever happened now – and she had no idea what that might be – at least she knew the truth and she knew she hadn't been a fool to love him.

"I'm sure," he said. "I've had years to prepare for this moment, and I feel turned inside out. I think ye can take a day or two to come to terms with meeting me again."

"I doubt if a day or two will be long enough for me to feel like my feet are touching the ground."

He spread his hands in appeal. "Won't you tell me what happened to ye? I've spent all these years picturing horrors. I kept imagining what a young girl might come to, lost in London."

It was her turn for a crooked smile. "Not what you've been thinking, at least."

She was well aware of how lucky she'd been. It was one of the reasons that she'd always be grateful to the people who had saved her. What anguish Malcolm must have endured, not knowing what had become of her. The compassion that wrung her soul was too ferocious to be called pity.

"Fearing what might have happened to ye has kept me from a decent night's sleep since you left."

That might sound like an overstatement, except that this man was exhausted, both emotionally and physically. And not just with a couple of days of hard riding in winter weather. Some trace of her earlier love must linger, because Rhona ached to take him in her arms and press his silvered head to her bosom. She longed to offer him some surcease from his troubles.

She couldn't do that. More than half her life had passed since she last saw him, and she'd spent all that time resenting him. She had to keep reminding herself that they were strangers, united only by the son he didn't know and those golden days when she was young and innocent and unaware of how much pain the world could inflict. She certainly had no right to touch him.

That fierce pity still speared through her. How she hungered to offer him a shred of comfort. The visceral power of that craving to ease his troubles surprised her. She'd imagined her affection for him was dead, just as dead as he'd once believed her to be. Now it was clear that her heart wasn't as closed to Malcolm Innes as she'd assumed.

When she stood up, she caught a flash of sharp disappointment in those dark eyes. He must think she meant to leave him, although his confession of how he'd devoted all these years to searching for her had set her world turning in a different direction.

Rhona needed time to take everything in, to match what she'd discovered with what had happened to her. But years of rage had melted away to nothing the moment she'd accepted that he'd never betrayed her, never forgotten her. She'd let go of her rancor as if it had never been.

Oh, Malcolm.

Once more, she thought of that lonely wolf ranging the forests, so sure he'd find no place in the pack. Expecting his brethren to snap and snarl until he disappeared back into the shadows where he belonged.

More of that painful pity cramped her heart. She told herself that meant nothing. She'd pity any creature who had braved such wretchedness. But she had a disturbing feeling that there was more to her reaction than that.

Her voice emerged as a husky murmur. "You'll get a better night's sleep in the house than you will in the stables."

"You're asking me inside?" He spoke as if the idea was beyond comprehension.

She packed the remains of his meal back into the basket. He'd eaten like he was famished. He was too thin. As a youth, Malcolm had been lean, but this man was whittled down to absolute essentials.

"If you'd like that." With every moment they spent together, she became more aware of what their separation had cost him. She was enough of a mother to be glad that he'd eaten every scrap of the stew. Patrick was built like his father, tall and possessed of whipcord strength, and her son ate like a horse.

"We're no' wed," he said in a neutral voice.

A mocking smile twisted her lips, even as the poignant truth struck her that if matters had proceeded according to her naïve hopes all those years ago, they'd be looking forward to a twentieth wedding anniversary in eighteen months.

"Patrick's here to lend us some propriety, and I've sent all the servants home for Christmas. The nearest neighbors are far enough away not to notice an extra body inside the house in the middle of a snowstorm. I think my reputation will weather any gossip, that is if there's any gossip at all."

Another of those bleak almost-smiles that threatened to break her heart. A heart that proved much more vulnerable to her first love than she wanted to admit. "Are ye sure?"

She didn't smile back. He was so unsure of his welcome. She supposed that given the greeting she'd offered him, that wasn't surprising. But he must know she'd forgiven him.

No, more than that. She'd discovered that there was nothing to forgive, although to her sorrow, there was still a universe of pain to regret.

She struggled to sound like the practical farmer she'd become over the last five years. "Malcolm, I'm offering you a bed in the house where you can sleep like a Christian. You can skulk out here in the stables if you like, but it makes no sense if you do."

"A stable is a suitable place to seek shelter at Christmas, though," he said in an expressionless voice.

Surprise made her blink. That was almost a joke. Perhaps he was easing into her company. "Because it's Christmas and I have room, I'll do the charitable thing and invite you into the inn."

He rose and reached to take the basket from her. She'd forgotten that instinctive chivalry, although it had been such an essential part of the boy she'd known.

Rhona had a sudden agonizingly poignant memory of how gentle and courteous he'd been with her girlish self, although he was the laird's son and she was a humble crofter's daughter. He'd always made her feel like the finest lady in the land.

He still did, it turned out.

"Well, in that case, I accept with pleasure. Thank you."

She'd forgotten, too, how tall he was. For a charged moment, she stood in his shadow. She'd managed her own life for years and wasn't used to feeling fragile and feminine, but something about Malcolm towering over her made her heart flip over in a way that hadn't happened since...

Since the last time she'd been with Malcolm.

How absurd. How unacceptable. Disquiet knotted her stomach. It seemed she was still susceptible to him, despite the gulf of years gaping between them. At thirty-five, she'd imagined she was well past the stage of going all fluttery over a man.

She'd imagined wrongly.

CHAPTER FOUR

*M*alcolm put on his greatcoat, his hat, and his gloves, and picked up his small valise and the empty basket. Rhona extinguished the lanterns, apart from the one she'd carried over with his dinner, a meal she'd delivered with such grudging resentment. At least she no longer looked likely to hit him with the nearest shovel.

Small concessions, all of them, but enough to set the blood singing in his veins. Hell, her mere presence was enough to make him feel like life was worth living.

She wrapped the thick shawl around her head. "Ready?"

"Aye."

Although when they left the barn, the force of wind-driven snow stole his breath and made him stagger. Dun Carron was much further north, and he'd assumed the weather here in the south would be kinder. How wrong he'd been. Patrick's talk of him getting lost in a snowdrift on the way to the inn turned out to be no exaggeration.

Rhona stumbled and before Malcolm remembered that he no longer had any right to touch her, he transferred the basket to the hand holding the valise and caught her arm.

"Hold onto me," he shouted above the howling wind.

He waited for her to argue. An hour ago, she would have cursed him to Hades for remaining on the property, let alone daring to touch her. But when he curled his gloved hand around hers, she returned his grasp.

An ember of warmth he hadn't felt in eighteen years sparked in his heart. Warmth that defied their frigid surroundings and a life that had taught him that while happiness was brief, suffering could last forever.

He battled to remind himself that he'd already fulfilled so many hopes today. It was greedy to want more.

But Malcolm did want more.

Although until he heard her story and discovered her present circumstances, he didn't know how much he could in good conscience ask for.

The yard wasn't huge, but crossing it felt like swimming the Atlantic. By the time he slammed the farmhouse door closed behind him, he was more aware than ever of the hard days of riding he'd done lately. He'd been on horseback since Fergus had come galloping up to Dun Carron.

Malcolm groaned and sagged against the door as comparative silence settled around them. "I'm damned glad Patrick took pity on me and didnae send me back onto the road," he said, fighting for breath.

Rhona watched him with a concentrated attention that he felt like a physical force. Her wariness hadn't entirely disappeared, although the hatred had faded, thank God. He still needed to come to terms with her spending all these years believing he was a faithless cad. Although his father in full flight as laird could be both convincing and terrifying, he supposed. If she'd swallowed that pack of lies his father had spun, it made sense that she hated Malcolm.

But in his heart, he couldn't contain his bruising disappointment. She should have trusted him.

At least she still held his hand. And to his surprise that lovely, lilting voice was warm when she spoke. "So am I."

Astonishment made him straighten. "Rhona..."

For a searing moment, wide green eyes locked with his and he could swear that he caught a trace of her old trust in those mossy depths. His grip tightened, and he started to draw her closer before he could remind himself of the dangers of wishful thinking.

She blinked and stiffened. What he thought he'd seen in her expression faded away – if it had ever been there at all. Worse, she tugged her hand free.

"Will you come through to the kitchen?" A quiver in the question told him she'd noticed his interest and it made her uncomfortable. "Patrick and I spend most of our time in there in the winter. There's a parlor for visitors, but I'd have to light the fire and even if I did, it's always cold. Although that's where we set up Christmas dinner."

He really had shaken her up. She was close to babbling with nerves.

"Och, the kitchen is fine." He told himself to be careful about rushing his fences. If today achieved no more than it already had, that should be enough after all these desolate years.

But that was the problem with hope. Once stirred into life, it started weaving dreams that he longed to make reality.

Counseling himself to patience, however difficult, he put down the valise and basket. He took off his snow-covered hat and coat and hung them on one of the pegs near the door. He noted the damp overcoat that Patrick had worn earlier. There wasn't another greatcoat.

Did that mean no other man lived here? Or did that indicate that the man who lived here was somewhere else and wearing his coat? In this violent weather, that lowering possibility was the more likely.

As Malcolm followed Rhona down a long black-and-white tiled hallway, he kept checking for evidence of a masculine presence, other than Patrick. All he saw was a cozy old house decorated with boughs of lush greenery for the season. The interior reeked of the same prosperity he'd noticed in the barn. With every step, the specter of Rhona starving on the streets of London receded.

That was something else he should be grateful to discover. His beloved didn't appear to be in any want. In fact, if what she'd said in the barn was true, she'd never been destitute and cold and alone. If the man who shared this house was responsible for that, Malcolm had no justification for hating the bastard.

The kitchen turned out to be a large, warm room, redolent with baking. A rich fruitcake sat on the stone workbench and rows of golden shortbread were arrayed on cooling racks across a huge old oak table, scarred with decades of use. Malcolm glanced around in pleasure, taking a deep breath of the pine scent rising from the greenery bedecking the room. He set the basket on the bench and the valise near the wall. "This is a home indeed."

Rhona took off the shawl and draped it over a wooden chair near the blazing fire. Her ruffled hair was beguiling, making her look less severe than she had when she'd first greeted him. "Thank you. I always thought Dun Carron had a warm atmosphere, too. Not that I saw much more of the big house than the servants' quarters and the great hall where your parents put on the estate Christmas parties."

He'd danced with Rhona at those parties, often enough to bring down his mother's censure on his head. As the heir, he was meant to partner all the estate's womenfolk, not just the winsome lass he fancied.

"Ye were always the belle of Dun Carron."

She was. Being the laird's son hadn't saved him from coming to fisticuffs with the local lads, who resented that bonny Rhona Macleod was so obviously smitten. It wasn't just his parents who had objected to his partiality for the prettiest girl in the glen. It wasn't just his parents who had predicted trouble ahead for the laird's son and the crofter's daughter.

At the time, neither that jealousy nor those predictions of doom had seemed to matter.

Malcolm should have paid more attention.

Rhona gave a dismissive wave and avoided his eyes. "You were always a flatterer."

Back then, he had been, in part because he loved to watch her get into a flutter at his extravagant compliments. Now so many years later, that lighthearted lad and lass seemed like characters in a play. Pretty dolls lined up in a nursery.

"Where's Patrick?" A few gaps in the rows of shortbread indicated the lad had sneaked in to sample his mother's baking.

"I'm guessing he's made himself scarce, in case I mean to box his ears for going behind my back and smuggling you into the barn." Such love weighted her tone that Malcolm suspected ear boxing was a rare occurrence. Whatever other suffering his son may have undergone, it was clear he'd never lacked a mother's affection.

"You'd have trouble reaching his ears. He must be a foot taller than ye."

It felt strange to tease Rhona. He hadn't teased anyone since that appalling day when they'd been ripped apart.

"He takes after his father." She didn't smile, although he noticed that she, unlike him, had preserved some lightness of spirit. "Please sit down. Are you still hungry?"

To his surprise, he was. For too long, eating had been a habit rather than a pleasure. "That shortbread looks good."

"Would you like tea? Or there's brandy in the cupboard if you'd prefer that. I wasn't expecting visitors."

He hid a wince at that description. Visitor! It needled that he couldn't claim a more permanent place in her life. He was determined to change that. At the very least, if Malcolm established a relationship with Patrick, Rhona would see a lot more of him.

"On a cold night so close to Christmas, brandy would be braw."

He sat at the table and pulled off his gloves as he watched her bustle around the kitchen. When she took off her gloves, he caught a glint from the band of gold on her fourth finger. Another kick to his gut. Another reminder that he needed to control his more primitive reactions.

She set out a plate of shortbread, before she pulled a bottle of brandy from the cupboard and poured two glasses. He hadn't expected her to drink with him. Reminder that this was a mature woman who had undergone experiences he didn't yet understand. That perhaps he'd never understand.

Something he hoped in part to remedy now. "How did ye survive in London? I swear I willnae judge you. I'm just glad you stayed alive."

She looked annoyed as she sat opposite him. "I already told you I didn't sell myself."

"You were so pretty, ye could have become a rich man's mistress."

"Well, I didn't."

He ignored her peppery response and sipped his brandy, surprised at the quality. He'd expected something fit only for cooking. Although what he'd most like was a dram of whisky. "Rhona, I'd dearly love to ken how you left me as a penniless crofter's daughter, yet here I find you with a flourishing farm, half of Scotland away from Dun Carron. I assume ye married. You're wearing a wedding ring."

"I did marry," she said in a flat voice.

That answer crushed any frail hopes Malcolm had that she wore the ring as a way to preserve appearances. It was a possible explanation. After all, she had a son to protect, as well as her reputation.

Again he told his masculine instincts to behave. They had no right to smart at the thought of her giving herself to another man. If that other man had saved her from poverty and prostitution, Malcolm should instead go on his knees and thank the lucky devil.

Although he wasn't quite so saintly, he struggled to keep his tone reasonable as he spoke. "Straightaway?"

The ironic glance she sent him indicated he failed. "Not far off. Patrick was born in wedlock, so on paper, he's no bastard."

Malcolm supposed that was a good thing, too, although every cell of his body howled in protest at some other man claiming the boy as his son. "Patrick knew about me, even if he didnae know my name."

There had been surprise and curiosity on his son's face when Malcolm turned up out of the snow, but more at the fact of his arrival than his existence.

"Yes, Patrick knew that I carried another man's child when I married my husband. Or at least I explained as much as I could to him when he was old enough to understand."

"Did he mind?"

"I think he must always have guessed something of the sort. He was one of those babies who was born wise."

A new fear gripped Malcolm. "His stepfather was unkind to him?"

Rhona shook her head, and a gentle smile unlike any Malcolm had seen so far tonight curved her lips. Her affection for the man she'd married was clear. Jealousy raked long, bloody marks across his heart.

"No, his stepfather was the best of creatures."

Malcolm shifted and clenched his fists on his lap under cover of the table. Again he reminded himself that he should be grateful that Rhona had fallen in with a good man.

"Where is this paragon?" He struggled to stifle his sarcasm. Yet again, he failed. "Are ye expecting him home for Christmas?"

Sadness deepened Rhona's eyes to malachite, and Malcolm felt small and unworthy, even before she answered. As he recognized her genuine grief, he squirmed in shame.

"Samuel died five years ago, down in London." She paused, as if reluctant to share the news with her former suitor. "I'm a widow."

CHAPTER FIVE

cross the table, Rhona watched more of the tension leach from Malcolm's face as she told him she was a widow. Which troubled her. After all this time, he shouldn't harbor hopes of making her his. For pity's sake, they were different people from those wide-eyed, fatally innocent children back in Dun Carron.

She'd grown up fast in London, a process that started even before that, with her cruel ejection from her home. She'd learned to read people, and men in particular. Malcolm was interested in her as a woman, whether out of sentimentality or curiosity to see who she'd become in their years apart. That quality of concentration he focused on her was unmistakable. This was a male setting his sights on a female he desired.

How did she feel about that?

She wasn't sure. She'd spent most of her adult life hating him with every beat of her heart, even as that same nitwitted heart had missed him to the point of agony. But the lad she missed had been the lad she'd loved at Dun Carron, and she'd convinced herself that he'd never existed outside her girlish fancies. The real Malcolm Innes was a lying, treacherous coward.

His arrival tonight had restored her vision of the boy she'd adored. Brave, honorable, steadfast. So steadfast that he'd spent years searching for her, and when he finally accepted she was dead, he'd searched for his son. She'd been smarter than she knew when she described Malcolm as Sir Galahad.

But the life of a questing knight was lonely and arduous, providing none of the more usual comforts of home or family. She thought again of that lone wolf skulking outside the pack, turning savage and rough with loneliness and yearning. This man who watched her with starving eyes wasn't the straightforward youth she'd fallen in love with. He carried an edge of risk and mystery.

She was certain that he wanted something from her. Something? She feared he wanted everything, even after all this time without her.

Rhona struggled to keep a level head, but it was more difficult than it should be. Malcolm was an attractive man, and something about the purity of his devotion appealed to the stupid, susceptible girl who lurked beneath the pragmatic farmer. If there were no other complications, she might even welcome him into her bed. It had been five empty years since Samuel died, and she'd missed a man's touch.

But there were complications. Enormous complications. Patrick's presence in the house for a start.

Not to mention that she could already tell that Malcolm didn't want one quick tumble to warm up a winter's night. He wanted what they once had.

And that couldn't be.

To return to what they'd once shared meant that she'd have to return to the person she'd once been. That girl had died at Dun Carron and been buried for good on the streets of London. It would take a Christmas miracle of gigantic proportions to resurrect her.

Confirming what her instincts screamed, that black gaze narrowed. "Is there someone in your life now?"

"Yes, he's over six feet tall and he looks like his father," she said shortly.

"No' Patrick." Malcolm made a dismissive gesture. "You know what I mean."

To her regret, she did. She frowned, wondering whether it would be wise to broach the subject of the physical attraction that stirred between them. She supposed it wasn't surprising that some of that old hunger lingered. Her younger self hadn't been able to keep her hands off Malcolm, and he'd been the same. Physical passion had swept her into a world where prudence held no sway. All that mattered were the glorious sensations her young lover could conjure from her body.

Well, what a cursed mess that had got them into. Although despite everything, Rhona couldn't regret having Patrick. He'd been a worry. He'd been a responsibility. But he'd never been less than a joy. He still was.

Sipping her brandy, she considered her response. "Malcolm, I don't know what hopes you're nurturing." Although, God help her, she did. She injected a steely edge into her voice. He needed to understand that after all this time apart, they couldn't take up where they left off. "But you must know that they can't come to fruition. All that unites us now is some painful history and an almost grown son. After everything that has happened, I'm surprised you're still such a romantic."

"I was always a romantic," he said, unperturbed by her warning.

"You were. To your detriment. After a few years of fruitless searching, any sensible man would have settled for a wife and family and a portion of happiness on his fine estates."

"Sensible!" he spat out, as if the word tasted disgusting. "I'd voyaged to the stars and back with ye. How could you think I'd settle for an earthbound existence, full of meat and potatoes?"

She tried not to feel flattered. Although she dared any woman not to find a morsel of gratification in hearing how deeply she'd scarred her first love's heart. "You can live on meat and potatoes."

"Ye can live on hope and memories, too."

She shook her head and indicated him where he sat, eating her up with his avid gaze. "Not by the look of you. You're worn down to the bone. You look like you haven't known one second of ease in twenty years. You look like a dog chained up in a yard and left to starve."

To her surprise, instead of greeting her unkind description with anger, faint humor lit his eyes. In truth, he looked less desperate than he had when he'd arrived. She guessed that a crushing burden had lifted off him when he discovered that both she and Patrick were alive. "Are you saying I'm no' handsome enough to take your fancy?"

She didn't smile. Partly because she was unwilling to admit that if she met him as a new acquaintance, she could fancy him indeed. This mature Malcolm had an intensity that drew her, a promise that this was a man who knew how to share pleasure beyond imagining with a lover.

Stop it, Rhona. You're not sixteen anymore. You more than most know the price the world extracts from people who surrender to their lusts without thought of consequences.

She kept the edge on her voice. "I'm saying you caused me a lot of trouble." Now there was an understatement. "I don't want you causing me any more. I've built up a good life. I won't have you marching in and turning that upside down."

That devouring black gaze didn't waver. She tried to ignore how that steady regard made her insides melt into treacle. "So do I have a rival?"

"There's no race," she snapped, pushing her chair back from the table and standing up to break the spell he cast over her.

How the devil did he do that? It wasn't that long ago since she'd wanted to crack him on the head with a poker and shove him back into the snow to freeze.

"That's what I'm trying to find out, Rhona. You nae longer have a husband. Has some local man caught your interest?"

She linked her hands at her waist. It seemed mad, but they showed a tendency to shake. "What if someone has?"

Plague take Malcolm. She was usually more adept than this at discouraging intrusive male interest. It was one of the first things she'd learned in London.

He sat back and folded his arms over his chest, forming a picture of aristocratic ease. "I'm just sizing up the opposition."

Annoyance flattened her lips. "I'm the opposition, damn you. You can't just waltz in here and start laying claim to a woman who you haven't seen in half a lifetime."

One of those expressive dark brows rose. "Can I no'?"

"No, you can't."

"Then why are ye getting in such a flap?"

"I'm not in a flap," she retorted, although she was. Even more annoying, Malcolm became calmer as she verged closer to losing her temper. It was as if with every moment in her company, his aims became more certain.

"Is there a suitor?"

"If there is, will you go away?"

"Dinnae be a silly goose." The black eyes glittered. "You know I won't."

There. Rhona was right to worry. She scowled at him, as her pulses skipped and stumbled with stirring trepidation. "You have no privileges here. In Muirburgh, the Laird of Dun Carron is just another traveler passing through."

More calmness, blast him. "I'm no' passing through."

That sparked her wrath. "Well, you're not staying. Once the snow clears, you're on your way, my fine bully boy. Right now I wish I'd left you in the barn."

"You probably do." Rueful amusement turned down his lips. "But I cannae go away. What about Patrick?"

It was a fair question. Now Malcolm had discovered his child, he'd be a constant presence in her life. For heaven's sake, they hadn't had a chance to discuss the matter yet, but Malcolm had said he intended to leave Dun Carron to her son. "You and he can sort things out between you."

Malcolm's expression turned serious, and he sat up straight. "You willnae try and stop us finding some way to go on?"

Rhona knew that she'd be more prudent to say that she would. But how could she deny her son the chance to know his father? Especially when that father now turned out to be a decent man. "Of course not."

Malcolm's expression eased another few notches. "Thank you. I appreciate that." His eyes sharpened on her face. "So tell me, Rhona, is there a lover?"

Her lips flattened with impatience. "You're not going to leave this alone, are you?"

"What do ye think?"

She gave a derisive snort. "I think, Malcolm Innes, that you've grown unpleasantly obstinate over the last years."

"I've always been obstinate." That annoying calmness persisted. "Over the important things at least."

He had been, she remembered with a shock. At least with what he cared about. Like her. Didn't she have proof of that right now? Only a man obstinate to the point of obsession would have kept looking for Patrick all these years.

Her sigh conveyed surrender. She could lie, she supposed. Although once Malcolm started spending time with Patrick, it would be inevitable that he learned that she slept alone. Even if she could convince Malcolm that she had a swain, he'd already said that made no difference to his plans to pursue her.

After she'd lost Malcolm, it had taken a long time for Rhona's broken heart to mend. Raging at him for letting her down should have helped to erase her longing. But it hadn't, even while she remained convinced that the man she missed like the very devil had only ever existed in her imagination.

But eventually she found a peace that was all the sweeter after the tumult preceding it. She was unsure that she wanted to jeopardize that peace. She liked Muirburgh. She liked running Burnside Farm. As the owner of one of the best spreads in the glen, she played a large part in local affairs. The people here had no idea of her past, and she liked that, too.

She sighed again and crossed to add more wood to the already blazing fire. It was an excuse to escape Malcolm's eyes. She didn't want to witness his triumph when she admitted the truth.

Her voice was low, but he was listening so intensely that she knew he'd hear her. She'd forgotten how powerful that pure focus was. Even as a boy, he'd paid careful attention. "No, there's no lover."

A silence fell. After a long while, she turned back to Malcolm. He was leaning back in his chair once more, and the brandy glass dangled from one long-fingered hand.

With his noble air and fine clothes, he should look ridiculous in this humble farmhouse kitchen. Instead he looked like a man who had found his place in the world at last.

Rhona struggled to summon some resentment at how at home he appeared. It was as if he already laid claim to a role as master of her house.

But it was hard to be angry, when his male beauty made her heart perform giddy somersaults. He wasn't at all the bonny laddie she'd fallen in love with, but there was a touch of danger and worldly experience to this man that she found exciting.

Heaven save her. She'd already made an utter fool of herself over Malcolm Innes. Surely she was old enough and smart enough to protect herself from his attractions now.

The awful truth? She wasn't sure she was.

"I thought you'd be dancing around the kitchen in celebration," she said in a sour tone, although she was more irked about her own weakness than she was with him.

That downturned smile reappeared. "Why don't ye have a suitor?"

"Do you want competition?" she asked sharply, noticing that he'd already wolfed down the shortbread she'd put out for him. She crossed and started to cut him a slice of cake, before she remembered she didn't want him to feel too welcome.

He'd gone back to staring at her as if he could read her soul. Once perhaps he could. No longer. Or at least that was what she told herself.

"You're a spectacular-looking woman. And you've become a person of some substance in this glen. I would imagine the single men of Muirburgh are pounding down the door to propose. No' just the single men, although the married ones willnae be offering a wedding ring."

She slid the plate of cake before him. "A few fellows might have expressed an interest."

More than a few. This was the first year she'd given all the farmhands the chance to go home for Christmas. In previous years, she'd kept a couple of them around the place to discourage any suitors who mightn't take no for an answer. She also had several guns in the house, and knew how to use them.

Rhona had been abducted once in her life. She never intended to be caught so helpless again.

After their courting failed to persuade her, the local men had become less persistent. With Patrick nearly grown, this year she'd given her workers a short holiday. The irony was that this year a genuine threat to her independence had come riding up the drive.

Although she already knew Malcolm wouldn't descend to violence. She'd spent enough time in the barn, watching him with the horses, to understand that the kind boy had grown up to be a kind man.

The discomfiting truth was that he didn't need to resort to violence. Nostalgia and his unassuming charm were more likely to seduce her into his bed than roughness ever could.

Even more discomfiting, she suspected he knew it.

"I'm sure you've been wooed within an inch of your life. Did that sharp tongue frighten them all away?"

"Not everyone appreciates a headstrong woman."

He gave a grunt of amusement. "You were always that. I remember ye pushing me into the loch when you were twelve and I tried to kiss you."

She paused on her way back to the bench and regarded him in astonishment. "I'd forgotten that."

His smile was more natural this time. She told herself she didn't care, but some corner of her heart softened to gooey caramel at the sudden sweetness in his expression.

"That was when I decided ye were the one for me."

"Better you hadn't," she said bleakly. She'd fallen for Malcolm's smiles years ago. She would not fall again.

He shook his head, and his jaw took on the stubborn line that started to make her anxious. "No, never say that. You're my fate, Rhona. Ye always were. We've been given a second chance. It would be churlish to waste it."

CHAPTER SIX

Malcolm watched Rhona's shoulders tighten in immediate rejection. She spoke in a rush. "Stop talking as if we're bloody Romeo and Juliet. We never had a chance together. These years apart have done nothing to change that."

She was wrong. Of course they had a chance. But he could see that it was still too early to convince her of that fact.

He wasn't as discouraged by her attitude as he could have been. He'd noticed her sidelong glances and the fluster beneath her implacable manner. It might be nearly twenty years, but he still knew enough to see that whatever else might have faded during their long separation, the physical attraction that had brought them together was as strong as ever.

He wanted her. It surprised him how much, although their love had always burned with carnal fire. He'd imagined that now he was older, spiritual need would consume earthier urges. But here in this warm kitchen, he was far too conscious of her beauty.

His fingers itched to undo the thick red hair confined in its practical bun. Every night since he'd lost her, he'd dreamed of touching her dewy white skin. He was afire to explore her fascinating female shape. The generous jut of bosom that her modest dress did so little to conceal. The graceful inward curve of her waist. The graceful outward curve of her hips.

As a girl, she'd been a luscious armful. She was still a luscious armful.

"Sit down and tell me where you've been all these years," he said peaceably and began to eat the slab of fruitcake. "Wherever it was, you've learned how to cook. This is delicious."

The young Rhona had done her best to run her father's house, but after her mother died when she was five, she'd grown up a rough and ready housekeeper. Something clearly the years had remedied. This neat, well-organized kitchen screamed efficiency and good housewifery.

She didn't move, and her gaze echoed her earlier hostility. "Is that it? 'We're destined to be together, and by the way this is a good cake?'"

He'd noticed that his composure disturbed her. He liked her disturbed, and not just because the flush in her cheeks and the flash in her green eyes reminded him of the girl he'd fallen in love with. When she was disturbed, she stopped trying to raise barriers against him and he caught a glimpse of her confusion and turmoil at meeting him again.

"It is a good cake," he said and pushed his empty plate toward her. "Could I please have another piece?"

It was odd. His awakened hunger for Rhona as a physical presence had awoken other physical needs. He'd tasted the food and the brandy with a kind of wonder. Both had a flavor and richness that he couldn't remember experiencing since he'd lost his beloved.

When she rolled her eyes, he wanted to laugh. He hadn't felt much urge to mirth in years either. Here in this snug kitchen, nigh on two decades of ice melted from his soul.

Although while he appreciated the homely comforts, it was the woman who made him feel like a living man again. Beneath his placid manner, a desperate fear stirred. If she exiled him back into the cold, what would he do? Losing her once had almost destroyed him. He wasn't sure that he'd survive losing her twice.

She turned to the bench and cut him an even bigger slice. She also cut herself a smaller piece. With an irritated bump, she set both plates on the table.

"Here. If you're staying for Christmas, I hope to heaven that I've got enough supplies in the larder to feed you."

Malcolm eyed her, reading how torn she was between irritation and attraction. "Am I staying for Christmas?"

"It's tomorrow. You'll be here for breakfast at the very least," she said grimly. She filled his glass with more of that excellent brandy and topped up her own glass as well.

"What a bonny thought."

He meant it. His parents had always kept a lavish Christmas, with parties for the crofters and neighbors. After Rhona had gone, he'd absented himself from the celebrations. Partly to punish his parents, partly because he couldn't bear all the jollity and goodwill when eternal winter reigned in his heart.

Since his father's death, he'd kept up the tradition of parties for the tenants, but he always made sure he was away. For him, Christmas was just another empty day in an empty life.

Malcolm decided to go on the attack about where she'd been all these years, or else she'd dodge the topic until doomsday. "How was it that I never found any trace of ye in London? I had an army of private agents looking for you. But Rhona Macleod had disappeared in a puff of smoke. I ken London is a big place, but I should have heard something."

Rhona sat down opposite him and tore her fruitcake into lumps without eating it. She avoided his eyes. "I changed my name."

He hadn't thought of that. He should have. "What to?"

"Sarah Ashley."

He frowned. "That's an English name."

"Yes."

Something tugged at the edges of his memory. "Was there no' an actress called Sarah Ashley?"

She raised her eyes to meet his, and as he stared into those green depths, he realized the astounding truth, although it made no sense. "Ye went on the stage."

"Yes."

"But you left Dun Carron with a thick Scottish accent. How the devil could ye make a career in the theater in London?"

Even he, wrapped up in grief and fear and anger, had heard of the famous Mrs. Ashley, the queen of Drury Lane. Not that her fame encouraged him to book a seat to see her. Entertainments such as the opera and the theater hadn't been part of his Spartan life.

"Clearly someone trained me in how to sound like a wellborn Englishwoman." She was watching him with more of that wariness, judging his reaction. "I told you before that I was only almost respectable.

A lot of people view actresses as little better than prostitutes."

He pushed away his empty plate and started to join together the pieces of what she told him. "This man ye married—"

"Samuel."

At last he had a name for the toad. "He was the one who trained ye."

"He saved my life," she said, without a hint of the theatricality that had apparently dominated her existence while Malcolm had been combing the slums looking for her.

"But you'd never expressed any interest in the stage," he said, still bewildered. If she had, he'd have remembered and tried to find her among London's acting companies.

"I was a crofter's daughter from the far corner of the kingdom. I'd never seen a play, let alone set foot in a theater when I got to London. I may as well have wished to fly as wished to become an actress." A familiar bitterness rasped in her voice. "Anyway, why should I wish to become an actress, when I already harbored the dream of loving you for the rest of my life?"

"You always had a lovely singing voice." She'd sung the solos at the local ceilidhs and in church. "And ye were a good dancer."

"At an amateur level. I needed lessons in both singing and dance before I made the grade, but I was a quick learner."

He wasn't surprised to hear that. He'd always admired her cleverness. She must have been a quick learner when it came to her elocution lessons, too. Mrs. Ashley was famous, yet he'd never heard a hint that she was born in Scotland.

What was frustrating was that the Theatre Royal was but a stone's throw from Seven Dials and

London's other slums. There must have been many occasions when he was mere yards away from her. The missed opportunities created an acrid weight of regret in his belly. If only he'd known!

"But you were pregnant when ye left Dun Carron."

"Yes."

"That must have interrupted your acting career."

"It did. But by that stage, I'd married Samuel."

Malcolm told himself not to be angry. She'd stayed safe, which meant he owed her husband a universe of gratitude.

She went on in a matter-of-fact voice, as though she didn't recount wonders. "Your father's money didnae last long in London, especially after someone stole my purse the day after I arrived. I tried everywhere, but I couldn't get work."

"Because of the baby?" Queasiness twisted his stomach, as he imagined how frightened and alone she must have felt.

She shook her head. "No. At that stage, the pregnancy didn't show, although if I'd found work, I would have had trouble keeping it, once people saw I was carrying a baby. I couldn't find work, because nobody could understand a word I said." She paused. "I'd only been in London a couple of days, but with every hour, I was more and more afraid. And while I kept my head down and tried to avoid attention, men had started to notice me. I had a few close calls."

Malcolm could imagine, although he didn't want to, damn it. "So what happened?"

Shame dulled her eyes, and he braced to hear the worst, despite her earlier assurances. "I decided that if people could steal from me, why couldn't I steal from someone else? I didn't owe the world anything, and being honest had done me no favors at all."

A relieved breath escaped him. "Ye turned pickpocket?"

He shouldn't feel too relieved. Theft was a capital crime, although pregnant women were in most cases transported to the hell of Botany Bay, instead of carried off to face the hangman. Not much of an improvement.

"I tried. But my first victim caught me in the act."

"And handed ye over to the magistrates?" Malcolm's earlier relief evaporated into horror.

She shook her head. "No. Although any other fellow would have. He was an older man, obviously well-to-do. He had no reason to take pity on me, but he did. He must have seen some potential in me. Instead of summoning the law, he took me to a chophouse and gave me my first hot meal in a week."

"And asked ye to be his mistress?"

"Not straightaway. First, he asked me to join his theatrical company as a dancer."

Her spectacular beauty had saved her. He was still jealous of Samuel, who had enjoyed her presence, while Malcolm had been going mad searching for her. But even through his cantankerous male reactions, some trace of reason told him that without Samuel, she'd have been in dire trouble. Likely she wouldn't have survived. That meant that Patrick wouldn't be alive today either.

She went on. "He invited me into his house."

"I'll bet he did," Malcolm said in a grim tone.

She cast him an unimpressed look. "It was all quite innocent. A lot of the company lived with him. I'm sure he took me on as an act of charity. At least at first. After a week on the streets of London, I was nothing much to look at."

Except that pure beauty would shine through dirt and hunger and poverty. Samuel Ashley must have known what a treasure he'd found.

"And he asked ye to share his bed?"

She sent him a disapproving look. "He was a good and generous man, and I believe he was acting out of a generous heart. It's too long ago for you to be jealous, Malcolm."

A thousand years wouldn't be long enough. But he reminded himself that he was a civilized man. At least on the surface.

Anyway, Samuel Ashley was dead, poor sod. Even if Malcolm wanted to knock his lights out, it was too late.

He drained his brandy, relishing its burn. "Go on."

When Rhona raised the bottle to pour him more, he shook his head. Not long after he'd lost Rhona, he'd sought oblivion in strong spirits, but they'd never helped. And the physical misery of emerging from a bout only made his situation more painful. He'd never adopted the habit of heavy drinking.

"Losing you devastated me," she said, and now she didn't sound like she told a story about someone else. Now she sounded like a woman who knew too much about sorrow. "I think my heart stayed frozen until Patrick was born. After that, my heart belonged to him."

So like her to go straight to the essence. "You loved Samuel."

"I honored him. I admired him. He was a good, kind man, and he was wonderful to me. And, yes, I loved him. Not as I'd loved you. I wasn't capable of loving anybody the way I'd loved you. When your father abducted me and convinced me that you'd seduced me with sweet lies, I wanted to die. If I hadn't been carrying Patrick, I would have given up."

Malcolm shook his head. "No, you wouldn't. You've always been a fighter. Even without Patrick, you'd never crumble into a heap and let life defeat you. I'm no' belittling your despair, but it's not in ye to surrender."

He should take comfort from that, even if she spoke of their love in a bleak past tense. But he couldn't help thinking how close he'd come to finding her. If he'd read any of the more gossipy papers, he'd almost certainly have seen a sketch of her. He'd have discovered that his lost love had become the celebrated Mrs. Ashley.

What then? Rhona had already wed Samuel. Malcolm could have no legal claim on her or his son. "Ye shared his bed."

Her mouth flattened. "I was his wife."

She'd never been Malcolm's wife, whatever he felt in his heart. "How did you come to marry him? You said he asked ye to be his mistress."

"He did, a month after I joined the company. To my surprise, I found I loved being on the stage, and I made friends among the other actors." Her eyes glowed with remembered excitement. And why not? Malcolm could imagine that being the celebrated Mrs. Ashley had been marvelous. Especially as she'd sailed so close to disaster before Samuel rescued her. "Thanks to Samuel, the men who hung around the theater kept their distance. Most of the time. Even better, I discovered I was good at what I did. I was a dancer for a week, then I had a few small speaking parts, despite my Scots accent, and a song or two. Within a month, audiences were noticing me."

"That cannae have gone down well with the other actresses."

She shrugged. "There was some jealousy, and the leading lady joined another company after a shrieking scene."

He could imagine. "So ye became the leading lady instead."

"I did. That's when Samuel invited me to be his mistress." She took a sip of her brandy. "I had to tell him that I was expecting your baby. I thought Samuel would throw me out on my ear, but he was a saint."

A saint who wanted Malcolm's woman for his own. It was an unworthy thought, he knew, but he couldn't help it.

Rhona continued. "He offered to marry me to give the child his name. Instead of going into a rage because I had to retire from the stage for a few months, he devoted that time to training me. He taught me to become the actress that Sarah Ashley eventually turned out to be."

Malcolm was almost becoming used to the fondness in her voice when she spoke of Samuel. "Ye enjoyed that."

"I did. I learned how to craft a performance and carry a company with me. It was magic becoming all these different women. Especially as I was so desperate to wipe out any trace of Rhona Macleod, the gullible ninny who had let Malcolm Innes make such a fool of her."

"You must have changed your name before ye married Samuel." Or else his agents would have heard news of her.

"I started on the stage as Sarah Gill. But Miss Gill's career only lasted a few weeks. After I gave birth to Patrick, I went back as Mrs. Ashley."

"So all up, ye had a career of, what, a dozen years or so?"

"A career uninterrupted by the arrival of more children." Sadness dimmed the light in her eyes. "Samuel would have loved a family, but it wasn't to be."

Malcolm had already guessed that there were no other children. If there were, they would be here with her now.

Her gaze remained somber. "Don't hate me for finding my way after we parted."

His gesture was dismissive. "Hate you? I'm in awe that ye became the toast of London."

Her expression didn't ease. "But you would have preferred me to be with you."

He shrugged, although he didn't take the matter lightly. "What can I say? Losing ye was like having a limb amputated. I've only limped through life ever since. I always wanted you with me. But that doesn't mean I cannae applaud the talent that saved you. I'd rather have you alive and well and happy with Samuel than dead in a garret somewhere, worn out with poverty and vice. I might be a selfish devil, Rhona, but I'm no' a monster."

A wry smile twisted her lips. "Yet still I feel I ought to apologize for my contentment."

"Don't," he said sharply, his fist clenching against the tabletop. "You lived. Patrick lived. Now I've found ye again." He forced himself to speak the words. It felt like his mouth was full of broken glass, but they had to be said. "Thanks to Samuel."

"Yes, thanks to Samuel," she said in a quiet voice.

A silence fell while Malcolm reminded himself of all he owed the man she'd married. His anger faded, his envy didn't. What a blasted lucky sod Samuel had been to have all those years with Rhona.

He sighed. "Finish your story. You still haven't told me how ye ended up in Muirburgh."

He couldn't mistake the sorrow shadowing her eyes. But he'd risen beyond his jealousy at last. Samuel had loved Rhona, too. He must have, to have treated her with such extraordinary generosity and to have discerned the burning soul of the artist within the starving waif who tried to rob him.

From the first, Samuel had been Rhona's savior. In fact, the nauseating truth was that Rhona's husband had done a much better job of protecting her than her young lover ever had.

"We had a run of good years, successful in business and happy at home. Samuel loved Patrick and was a wonderful father to him."

"You can see that when ye meet Patrick," Malcolm said.

"Yes, you can," Rhona said in that soft tone that always made Malcolm's bones melt.

He'd spent an eon living with no touch of affection to soften his isolation. He was magnanimous enough to be thankful that love had surrounded both his darling and his son. He wouldn't wish the hell of his last years on his worst enemy. And Rhona was far from that.

She went on. "Samuel was fifty when we married." That wry humor reappeared. "Onstage, he always played my father. When his health failed, I stopped acting, so I could nurse him. Luckily, we'd made good money while we worked together."

"A dozen years of full houses as Londoners flocked to see the superb Mrs. Ashley."

"Our company was the fashion." She paused. "Samuel died five years ago. I could have gone back to my career, I suppose. Everything was in place for me to take over the company. While Samuel was sick, the actors toured under a manager. But losing Samuel took away my enthusiasm for acting, and I didn't want Patrick to grow up in London. Nobody knew I was a good Scots lass. But I knew, and I wanted to come home."

"So ye bought a farm and settled near Loch Lomond. Did you never think of coming back to Dun Carron?"

She shook her head, and a faint bitterness darkened her face. "Dun Carron holds too many painful memories. Even if your father would let me settle there. As far as I knew, he was still alive and in charge. And how could I take Patrick to a place where everyone would recognize him as Malcolm Innes's child? Better my son and I retired to a place where we could make a new start. Me as a respectable widow with no connection to old scandal or to the notorious stage."

"I don't care what the world says about ye." He never had. Now even less than ever. "I take my hat off to you. Your courage makes me want to cheer."

She eyed him as if suspecting some trick, but his admiration was sincere. "I did what I had to."

His hand sliced the air, dismissing her self-effacing response. "You did more than that. You created something magnificent out of pain and failure. My father had it so wrong when he said I was too good for ye. You're too good for me. You always were."

"Malcolm, I..." She looked stricken, although he hadn't meant to upset her.

He spoke before she could argue with him. "It's been a night of overwhelming revelations." He dared to tell her what he intended, although he knew he risked ruining their uncertain truce. "Dinnae make any decisions now. Sleep on it. But I'd like to court you, Rhona. I always wanted ye to be the lady of Dun Carron."

Her expression turned stormy, and her hands bunched on the table. "What if I don't want to be courted?"

He stared at her steadily, seeing so much that had changed from the girl he'd loved and so much that stayed the same. "Are you saying ye feel nothing for me?"

Rhona waved a despairing hand and stood to clear away the plates and glasses. She looked spent, not just physically but spiritually. He felt much the same. Too many impossible dreams had come true tonight. The way his life had changed in the space of mere hours left him reeling.

"I don't know what I feel."

That wasn't true. The sexual awareness vibrating between them was almost visible. But he didn't push for confessions. Tomorrow they'd talk again. More, he'd have a chance to spend time with Patrick, God willing.

And it was Christmas. If ever there was a time for wishes to be granted, it was Christmas. The signs were good. For the first time in eighteen years, Malcolm was spending the holy festival with people he loved.

CHAPTER SEVEN

Malcolm lay awake in the comfortable room that Rhona had shown him into. A fire blazed in the hearth, and he stretched out under a pile of eiderdowns in a big oak bed.

The snowstorm seemed to have blown itself out. The house around him was silent, and he was drained, not just from the last few days, but from years of bracing to discover the worst.

Whatever happened next, his obsessive searching had reached a happier outcome than he'd ever dared imagine. Even if Rhona decided she couldn't bear to see him again and Patrick evinced no interest in his long-lost father, the world was a brighter place now that Malcolm knew that both Patrick and Rhona remained in it.

Yet still he couldn't sleep. His head was buzzing with Rhona's astonishing story. How marvelous she was. If only he could tell his stiff-necked father just what a treasure he'd scorned all those years ago. She was unlike anyone else, a queen and a goddess.

He'd cherished the memory of the young Rhona, but already the woman she'd become, so much more complex and fascinating, encroached on that image. His faithful soul was doubly pledged to her. Even with Rhona doing her best to maintain the distance between them, he'd tasted something like happiness in her kitchen tonight. The nearest he'd come to happiness since she'd left him.

He'd found Rhona. He'd found Patrick. Surely heaven wouldn't be malicious enough to snatch away this second chance at fulfillment.

Except his trust in heaven's benevolence had come to a violent end when he was eighteen. He couldn't accept that now he'd found his beloved and his child, they wouldn't disappear again. How unbearable to think that Rhona might send him back into the cold. In these last years, he'd barely clung to a scrap of humanity. What little remained of the man he'd once been would disintegrate if there was to be nothing more between him and Rhona than one short evening of prickly conversation.

She'd answered his curiosity about where she'd been all this time. But his needs stretched far beyond mere curiosity. None of which he could satisfy after midnight in this house where she'd offered him such grudging shelter.

Malcolm punched his pillow and shifted yet again on the soft featherbed. He told himself he hadn't had a good night's sleep since his darling had been ripped away from him, so what did it matter if he missed out on yet another? But on those frustrating, miserable nights, his love hadn't been sleeping a few doors along the corridor.

A good portion of his restlessness stemmed from frustrated desire. Over the years, it was inevitable that the Rhona in his mind had lost some of her physical reality. But tonight, seeing her in the flesh – and what glorious flesh it was – reminded him how a glance from those green eyes had once made him as randy as a young bull.

He was no longer a young bull, but, by God, his body didn't seem to recognize that reality. His body knew that paradise lay closer than it had in half a lifetime, and it was afire to bridge the distance.

Shifting onto his side, he wondered what time Rhona and Patrick got up in the morning. Malcolm might starve to touch her when he was with her, but that was still easier than being locked away without her.

Go to sleep, Malcolm. You can't go blundering around the house, hunting for her. You don't even know which room is hers. Not to mention that you want to convince her you're good husband material. Forcing your way into her room and begging her to take you into her bed won't make the best impression.

He closed his eyes on another sigh and tried to find a comfortable place in the bed. Although his restiveness had nothing to do with the bed and everything to do with the sexual excitement fizzing in his blood.

When the door opened, he wondered if he had in fact fallen asleep and was caught up in a dream. The flicker of a candle revealed Rhona in a white flannel nightdress, with the plaid shawl flung around her shoulders. Her rich red hair was confined in a single plait that draped across the lush curve of her bosom.

His pulse racing with wicked anticipation, Malcolm pushed up in the bed. "Rhona?" Then common sense asserted itself. "Is something wrong?"

She shook her head and stepped into the room, shutting the substantial oak door behind her. Malcolm's heart crashed against his ribs and stole his breath. He'd been alone with her for most of the evening, but there was something particularly evocative about her entering his bedchamber.

"I don't want Patrick to know I'm here," she whispered.

"Do ye want to talk some more?" He kept his voice to a murmur.

Her gesture expressed an uncharacteristic helplessness. "No."

Frowning, he worked through the implications of that. "Have ye come to throw me out into the snow, now the storm has passed?"

While he and Rhona hadn't ended the evening exactly as friends, she'd seemed to accept his presence in the house. But he couldn't forget the hatred in her eyes when he'd first arrived. Perhaps now she'd had time to reflect on his plan to court her, she'd decided she was better off banishing him from her presence.

She looked shocked. "Of course not."

Malcolm supposed that was something. He sucked in a relieved breath and recalled that he was naked. Her gaze fastened with unmistakable interest on his bare chest. The candlelight wavered as her hand trembled.

Now, that was interesting. Very interesting indeed. "Then what are ye doing here?"

She set the candle on top of the chest of drawers, and it was her turn to suck in a deep breath. "Actually I don't know. It's not for—"

"Bed sport?"

She avoided his eyes, and he wondered if she was blushing. The light wasn't bright enough to tell. Young Rhona had gone red as a rowanberry. Tenderness pierced his heart at the thought of this sophisticated woman blushing like the innocent lass she'd once been.

"No." She paused. "Not with Patrick in the house."

Malcolm's heart took off on another of those dizzying leaps. That sounded even more promising. Did that mean that if Patrick wasn't in the house, she might consent to take him into her body?

She made another of those helpless gestures. "I couldn't sleep."

"Neither could I."

"It's mad, but it felt wrong that you were so far away."

"It does."

"So I wondered if I can lie down beside you." She paused. "Just lie down."

He summoned a smile, although turbulent emotion churned in his gut. This was the first time she'd admitted that she recognized the bond linking them. "I understand."

She gave a huff of wry laughter. "I wish to heaven I did."

"Should I put on some clothes?" He pushed the bedcovers lower. "I'm no' wearing anything."

He bit back a groan while her eyes traced a searing path down his body, revealed now to the base of his belly. As she completed that leisurely inspection, she could have no idea how hunger sharpened her features.

His cock stirred, and he hoped to hell that she didn't guess his disquiet. After all these years without her, if she lay beside him, even without the possibility of congress, it would feel like a gift. He didn't want his powerful masculine urges to frighten her away.

She blinked and glanced away, as if she realized how her avid curiosity betrayed her. "Perhaps...perhaps that might be a good idea."

When she turned her back, a sardonic laugh escaped him. "Ye have seen me naked before."

"That was another lifetime," she said, and the sadness in her voice quietened his burgeoning excitement.

"Aye, it was." He rolled out of bed and with shaking hands tugged on his breeches. "You're safe to look now."

She turned to watch him slide back into bed. He held his hand out. "Come here, Rhona."

After she bent to blow out the candle, the fire provided enough light for him to watch as she unwrapped the shawl from around her and let it fall to the floor. The unselfconscious grace of the movement made the breath catch in his tight throat.

Gingerly, she slipped into the bed and lay flat as he pulled the covers over her. "May I hold ye in my arms?"

"You won't—"

"No, you have my word." He struggled to explain something that he didn't fully understand himself. "I want ye. You must know that."

"I supposed."

"But I want more from ye than just a quick tumble."

"It might be easier if a quick tumble was all you wanted." Regret weighted her voice.

Malcolm sighed and shifted onto his side. It was difficult to believe that he was so close to the woman he'd assumed lost to him forever. "How do ye like to sleep?"

It seemed absurd that he had to ask, given she'd borne his child and the memory of her had shadowed most of his life.

For years, he hadn't thought back to those joyous, innocent days when they'd both learned about love's pleasure. In the midst of his despair, dwelling on what they'd done to each other at Dun Carron had gouged a hole into his heart. But now he'd finally found her, he could revisit those sweet encounters, without grief and anger poisoning the memory.

That last summer before disaster struck, he'd spent hours lying in the sun with Rhona, learning what she liked and seeking his own delight, as well. Hours brilliant with light and love and laughter.

Her mind must be running along similar lines. "We did so much with each other, so many things we shouldn't, but we never shared a bed, did we?"

"No." They'd lain together in the lush summer grass of a hidden dell, lost high in the hills encircling the castle. He remembered 1806 as a summer without rain, although because this was Scotland, that couldn't be true.

"I used to dream of holding ye all night. I longed for the day I made you my wife, when I could carry you back to my room at the castle and at last claim you without secrecy."

A crushing silence descended. She, too, must be counting the many things they'd missed out on. Not least his chance to see his son grow up to become the fine young man he was today.

Malcolm raised a barrier against that thought. It promised to break a heart that had already broken too many times before. Tonight wasn't the time for bitter regret. Tonight was the time to give thanks that after all his searching, he'd finally found Rhona and Patrick. What happened next was still to be decided, but right now it should be enough that she was here beside him.

"I usually sleep on my side," she said, after a long, oppressive hiatus, burdened with too many thoughts of what might have been.

"Me, too."

After an interval of awkward maneuvering, they ended up with Rhona's back pressed into his chest and her head resting on the arm he curled beneath her. Lying like this, it would be so easy to cup those soft breasts. But Malcolm knew better than to tempt fate's mercy. And Rhona's forbearance.

He was devilish glad that she'd told him to put some clothes on. His breeches lent him a modicum of modesty. All this wriggling around played merry hell with good intentions.

Malcolm shifted his hips so she didn't feel his hardness pressing into her luscious rump. Since the day she left, he'd dreamed of having her with him again. He didn't want to give her any excuse to run back to her room. It might be excruciating to preserve the chaste contact, but it was better than sleeping alone.

Not that he'd been sleeping when she arrived. Not that he expected to sleep now.

"Better?" he asked softly.

"Better."

He buried his face in her hair, wishing he had the right to undo that luxuriant fall of red. When they'd come together during those sun-kissed afternoons at Dun Carron, her wealth of silky hair had cascaded around their straining bodies.

Malcolm breathed deep, taking in her rich scent. She smelled of herbs and shortbread and essence of Rhona. That elusive scent had haunted him most of his life. He hadn't expected it to be so familiar, even though her fragrance had twined its way through his lonely dreams.

She remained tense under his touch, although he was careful to keep his hands on her arms. He rubbed his face in her hair and dared to kiss her crown before he raised his head. "You're no' comfortable."

"I'm just a little nervous."

She didn't need to tell him. He heard the rapid flutter of her breath and felt the way she trembled in his hold.

"I told you I willnae make any demands on you tonight."

He chose his words with care. Beyond tonight, he wasn't promising anything. He needed to express his love physically. Before he went insane with wanting her, he hoped she might come around to the same opinion.

"I know. I believe you." She shifted, and he bit his lip to hold back a gasp, even as that tentative expression of trust settled in his heart and ignited a warm glow.

Somewhere deep inside, she still knew him, recognized him as her match. He hoped to hell that the recognition wasn't buried too deep. It would be a sodding tragedy if her desire never saw the light of day. "Thank you."

She went on in a tentative voice. "But it's five years since I lay in a man's arms. Even longer since the man touching me was you."

He stifled a long sigh of satisfaction. So there had been no other lovers apart from Samuel. Malcolm didn't have any right to gloat over this confession, but he was man enough to like hearing that she'd slept alone since her husband's death.

"Do ye want to go?" By God, it hurt to say those words, but he wanted her to understand that he had no intention of curtailing her freedom, even if she wed him.

Rhona as a girl had been headstrong and willful. From what Malcolm saw, those qualities had only become more pronounced in the woman. He'd always liked her spirit. He liked it even more now, after discovering that her strength of character had ensured her survival. A weaker woman would have succumbed to her evil circumstances.

He nearly died of suspense before she answered. "No."

Malcolm sucked in a relieved breath and decided to shut up before he said something that sent her scurrying.

For a long time, they lay like strangers, but gradually her rigidity eased. She shifted again and stretched her legs out along his. He tightened his grip on her and by accident brushed her breast through the flannel.

Arousal rushed through him. And dismay. For the first time in years, he felt warm. More, he sampled a fugitive peace. Although peace was a strange companion, when he was as hard as a damned flagpole.

She made a sleepy protest, but praise every angel in heaven, she didn't get up and leave.

After a hesitation, she snuggled back into him and whispered, "Merry Christmas, Malcolm."

He supposed it must be well after midnight. "Merry Christmas, *mo chridhe*."

Malcolm waited for her to object to the endearment, but she remained silent. A few minutes later, her steady breathing told him that she indeed slept. Another sign of trust.

Moisture stung his eyes as he stared unseeing into the firelit darkness. He blinked the tears away, even as poignant gratitude found a place in his lonely heart.

Life had been flat and gray for so long. For years, Christmas had turned into just another flat, gray day in a barren landscape. Whatever happened after this, he would have tonight. At this moment, he didn't even overly mind that he and Rhona lay side by side, like brother and sister.

His love was alive and with him. His love had come to him and offered her warmth to melt the chill that had ruled his world since she'd gone.

He heaved a deep sigh, tinged with her delicious scent, and cuddled closer to Rhona. She gave another of those drowsy murmurs and curled her hand over his where it had settled on her hip.

He refused to sleep. He didn't want to miss a second of this night.

And on that thought, he slept.

CHAPTER EIGHT

When Patrick appeared the next morning, Rhona was sitting in the kitchen, enjoying a cup of tea in front of the fire. He was a young man now, and one she was proud to call her son. But at times like this when he was all untidy hair and sleepy eyes, she couldn't help remembering the sweet toddler who had always been so happy to see his mother.

He bent to kiss her cheek. "Happy Christmas, Ma."

"Happy Christmas, Patrick," she said, hugging him, then pulling back to smooth the lock of hair sticking up above his forehead. "You're up early."

His pointed glance made her wonder if he guessed that she hadn't spent the night in her own bed. The blood rose to her cheeks. She'd always been a martyr to blushing. She'd hoped she might grow out of the affliction. She'd hoped in vain.

"So are you," Patrick said in a neutral voice.

Rhona lifted her cup to her lips to hide her embarrassment. She suspected she hoped in vain there, too. She was up early because she didn't want her son to know she'd slept with Malcolm. Even if that phrase held only its most innocent meaning.

Except that wasn't the full truth. Oh, Malcolm had kept his word and treated her with a chivalry that had filled her heart with tenderness. But she'd woken to find his hand curled around her breast and his leg thrown over hers. His body was pressed against her back and his rich scent surrounded her, enough like the scent of the boy she'd loved to make her feel safe and cherished.

Which was dangerous in itself. It would be so easy to drift into a sentimental dream, where she and her first love picked up where they'd left off. But that was impossible. They were different people, and it had been so long since they were lovers. How could whatever had brought them together in the first place survive all the pain and separation?

But however she arranged the future, in the here and now, Malcolm's arrival had stirred her dormant carnal needs to life. Even if she disregarded their past, Malcolm was an attractive man. And she was attracted. Powerfully so. The breast he'd cupped with such gentleness had swelled with longing, and her nipples had formed hard points, begging for a man's touch. For Malcolm's touch. The hot, heavy weight in the base of her stomach might have been long absent, but now it returned and she recognized the restless demands of arousal.

She'd found it far too difficult to leave that warm bed and that sleeping man without waking him to seek satisfaction. It might be best if she sent Malcolm on his way today, before she made a fool of herself over him yet again.

But as she'd stood over the rumpled bed and stared down at the man who had held her in his arms all night, her heart had sorrowed over what she saw.

Asleep, he looked vulnerable and drawn, and there was no chance of mistaking him for the beautiful boy she'd once adored. Even in slumber, his thin face showed the marks of strain, and the thick, silvered hair told its own tale of what these last years had cost him. She'd found herself blinking back tears of pity for all he'd endured. Worse, she'd had to fight the urge to crawl back into bed and take him in her arms.

She could imagine where that would lead.

So she left him to sleep. He was so deep in oblivion that when she left the room, he'd only made a drowsy murmur without surfacing to awareness. She'd come out to sit by the kitchen fire and give herself a lecture. A lecture laden with dispiriting common sense, about what a disaster it would be, to try and turn back the clock to a boy and girl who no longer existed.

"Would you like some tea?" she asked Patrick, setting down her cup and lifting the pot.

"Yes, please." Patrick brought a cup and saucer across from the dresser and watched as she poured for him. "I'm going into the church to practice my solo. The storm seems to have passed, so I shouldn't have any trouble getting to the village."

Patrick had inherited her talent for singing, and he'd become a mainstay of the Muirburgh church choir. Because he was such an important part of the seasonal services, she and her son usually postponed their Christmas celebrations until the midday meal. Then they celebrated in the English style, eating roast goose and plum pudding and exchanging presents. Most years, Rhona traveled into the village with Patrick for the early service, then came home to cook.

She rose and crossed to lift a heavy frypan from a hook on the wall. "You'll have breakfast first?"

"No, thank you. I slept too late for that. I'll take some fruitcake. That will have to do. Are you coming to church this morning?"

Rhona noticed that they were both very careful not to mention that a man was asleep in her guest bedroom. She put down the pan. "Not this year."

Patrick's searching stare reminded her that he wasn't a child anymore. "Are you going to ask my father to stay for Christmas dinner?"

Oh, dear, the subject was broached, forcing her to stop pretending that this was a Christmas like any other. "Would you like me to?"

"Yes, I would." Patrick's gaze remained steady. "But then, I don't have anything like your history with him. If you still hate him, I'll understand if you don't want him to stay."

"I don't hate him. It turns out I misjudged him all these years. He never stopped searching for us."

"Then I'm glad he found us."

Rhona had told Patrick that the man who had fathered him had deserted her, but nothing much beyond that. "He should tell you his story."

"And you should tell me yours. I don't know much more than that you're Scottish and you came to London to seek your fortune."

"Not exactly," she said with a grim twist of her lips. "Oh, the Scottish bit is true. But I had no choice in coming to London. I fell in love with the laird's son on the isolated estate I grew up on. His parents didn't like the idea of an ignorant crofter's daughter marrying the heir, particularly after they discovered I was carrying you. So they arranged my abduction. Until last night, I thought Malcolm had also been in favor of getting me out of the way. It turns out that his father locked him in the dungeons to stop him following me."

"Dungeons?" Patrick picked up on the least important part of what she'd said, reminding her that the child still existed inside his tall body. Her son was young enough to find the idea of dungeons romantic.

"Yes. Malcolm is the Laird of Dun Carron, and he lives in a castle."

Patrick sent her a direct look. "So he really is a questing knight."

Rhona gave a wry laugh. "Where do you get your imagination?"

Her son looked unimpressed. "Perhaps from my father. Do you think I can visit Dun Catherine—"

"Carron." It should feel odd to hear Patrick call Malcolm his father, but instead it felt right.

"...and see this castle?"

Given Malcolm's intention to make Patrick his heir, Rhona would pretty much guarantee it. But that piece of news was for Malcolm to deliver, not her. "I'd say it's likely."

"Capital." Patrick sobered, proving that the grown-up was there inside him, too. "And you were only my age when this happened."

Rhona was always fascinated with the way he was maturing. Watching him change from that affectionate toddler to this kind and clever young man was the greatest joy of her life. A joy she was aware that life had stolen from Malcolm. She'd been luckier by far in their separation than he had.

"Seventeen."

"You must have been terrified."

"I was. I'd never been to Inverness, let alone Edinburgh. London was a horrifying monster, full of people I couldn't understand and who didn't understand me. Without Samuel, I dread to think what would have happened. I'd never been anywhere that I didn't know every single person who lived there."

"Samuel was a good man."

"He was."

In the silence that followed, she felt Samuel's benevolent ghost hover close. He'd loved having all his acting company and friends around him at Christmas. If his soul lingered, it wished her no ill, she knew.

Patrick looked troubled. "Samuel would want you to be happy."

"I am happy."

"You're lonely."

Rhona was surprised that he'd noticed. She kept busy, and on her good days, she achieved a simple contentment, but it wasn't the same as having someone she loved to share her joys and her troubles. "I have you."

"You know what I mean."

To her regret she did, although Patrick had never been very keen on any of the men who had courted her. "Don't start knitting up happy endings, Patrick."

He paid no heed to her warning. "What does my father want? Does he mean to marry you and carry you back to his keep and make you the Lady of Dun Carron?"

Her laugh held an artificial note that she hoped her son didn't pick up. Because that was exactly what Malcolm did want, as mad as it sounded when they hadn't spoken a word to each other in eighteen years. It seemed her son's romantic imagination did indeed come from his long-absent father. "We're strangers."

"You didn't seem like strangers last night."

"You only saw us exchange a couple of words – and for my part, the words were 'get out.'"

Patrick didn't smile, although she'd tried to inject a mocking note into her answer. "It was enough. And you spent a lot of time last night talking to him."

"Were you eavesdropping, you dreadful brat?"

He shook his head, although he did smile at her calling him a brat. "No. But you were a long time in the stables and even longer in the kitchen, and it was late when you put out the lights."

"While you were skulking in your room to avoid a stern talking-to."

He rolled his eyes. "You're never that stern."

It was true. Thank goodness for the intrinsic sweetness of Patrick's nature, or else he would have become the brat she called him. He just had to look at her with those bright black eyes and she was putty in his hands. Even worse, he knew it.

He watched her now with more curiosity than trepidation. "My father wouldn't have made it to the inn through the blizzard. And you've forgiven me for asking him to stay anyway. If you hadn't, you wouldn't have taken him supper or let him sleep in the house."

"We cleared up a lot of misunderstandings last night."

"I'm glad. You seem...lighter this morning, as though you've put down a crushing load."

Rhona wasn't sure she liked her son directing this level of perception at her. A lot of her thoughts right now weren't suitable for him to guess.

He was right about one thing. These last years since Samuel fell ill and died and she'd made the move to Scotland had been full of hard work. She'd started to feel like she was wholly a mother and a farmer. Malcolm's arrival reminded her that she was a woman as well, and one not past the stage of experiencing a thrill at a handsome man's interest.

The problem was that the handsome man in question brought a lifetime of complications in his wake. He might look at her with a desire that made her blood pump faster than it had since she was a girl. But she and Malcolm could never come together free from the burden of their history.

She spoke in an airy tone to try and distract Patrick from looking too closely and divining the sinful impulses that Rhona harbored toward Malcolm. "That's because it's Christmas. I'm always happy at Christmas."

That wasn't true. When she'd first married Samuel, Christmas had been a reminder of everything she'd lost when she was banished from Dun Carron. But by the time Patrick was old enough to understand what the festival was all about, she'd come to love her small family and the unconventional theater people who crowded into her house to celebrate this holy day.

Patrick wasn't to be put off. "It's more than that. It's like you've given up something that has weighed you down all your life." He paused. "Hating the man who gave me life can't have been easy. Especially when every time you looked into my face, you must have remembered him."

Rhona regarded her son in horror. "No, Patrick, I could never hate you."

His smile was easy with confidence. "I know you love me, Ma."

Relieved, she felt her shoulders lower to a more relaxed line. "That's good. Because I do." She paused. "And you're wrong about my hatred being destructive. It was far too easy for me to hate Malcolm. It served to keep me from breaking my heart in grief. It's a long time ago now, but we were very much in love when we were young. It took me years to get over the separation."

"Now you have no reason to be bitter."

Oh, the innocence of youth. She remained furious with Malcolm's parents, and with her father for being so spineless when it came to protecting his daughter. She was still devastated that Malcolm had spent his life searching for them and wasting his remarkable capacity for happiness in sorrow and isolation. She was angry that he'd never had a family and a chance to discover the day-to-day pleasures she'd enjoyed with Samuel and Patrick.

Hmm. Perhaps she wasn't quite so angry about that last. Although if she was the sort of woman she'd like to think she was, she should be.

But while in the abstract, she might want Malcolm to find contentment without her, something in her relished the knowledge that he'd never stopped loving her. That same weak something positively crowed with triumph that he'd never found another woman he wanted to wed.

Oh, dear, it was clear that the Christmas spirit needed to do a bit more work on her unworthy self.

"You know, I do feel better," she said, which given her turmoil over her reunion with her first lover was an enormous surprise. Perhaps carrying around all that unresolved resentment had affected her more than she'd realized.

Patrick laughed. "I'm pleased to hear it." The clock on the mantel chimed half past six. He gulped down his tea, although it must be cold by now. "I'd better go. You didn't say if you're going to invite my father for Christmas dinner."

Rhona caught a fleeting glimpse of something she should have expected but which nonetheless startled her. Patrick was avid to know his father.

She supposed she couldn't blame him. This was his chance to discover where he came from. All his life, she'd done her best to give him security and love.

Now she saw that she'd never been able to supply the one thing that he longed for – a father who shared his blood.

Patrick's pleading black gaze had its usual effect. And today was Christmas. It seemed an act of unforgivable meanness to exile Malcolm to a lonely lunch at the inn, when he'd already been lonely for so many years. "Of course he can stay."

The relief in Patrick's smile betrayed how much her cooperation mattered. "And tonight perhaps you can tell me just what happened in Scotland all those years ago."

Rhona supposed he had a right to know that, too, although she wasn't quite ready to confess every youthful sin to her son.

After Patrick left, she made another pot of tea and sat down before the fire. Once she dressed, she had to check the animals, but that wasn't urgent. Yesterday, she and Patrick had made sure that the livestock had water and plenty of fodder. Yesterday, when she'd imagined that this was going to be a Christmas like all the others she'd spent at Muirburgh. Even on Christmas Day, a farmer's work never stopped. But Rhona always organized things so the holiday meant light duties.

Then she had to get the dinner on. Patrick would be starving when he got home, if he started the day with only a piece of fruitcake. He was always starving anyway. She often looked at that lanky body and wondered where all the food went.

Malcolm had been a similarly long and lean stripling, although over the years, he'd filled out to fit his frame. Too well for her peace of mind. Despite his thinness, that strong, sinewy body was hard and masculine and virile. Last night when she'd seen his bare torso, she couldn't take her eyes away from him, and her palms had itched to discover just how his skin would feel under her hands.

She'd learned to see Patrick as an individual, separate from the man who she believed had betrayed her. But it was still a shock to confirm how much her son looked like his father. Not to mention how much like Malcolm he was in other ways. The expressions on his face, his gestures, the tone of his voice, the way they both lounged in a chair with catlike grace.

Patrick was right about one thing at least. Giving up her hatred had freed her in so many ways, not least in her willingness to see her son as the product of the love she'd given his father.

She sighed and finished her tea and the piece of shortbread she'd picked up. The house was silent, which meant Malcolm must still be asleep. She was glad he had a chance to rest. It hurt to imagine what life had been like for him, as he'd searched as far as America for her and his son. No wonder he looked like he'd been tested to the limits. She was also glad that this Christmas had gifted her with the chance to discover the truth about those tragic events back in Dun Carron.

And perhaps, just perhaps, she might be glad that Malcolm was here on his own account, although she suspected her productive, quiet life on this farm might never be the same.

It took Rhona a bit more than an hour to organize the dinner. She'd done a lot of the preparations over the last few days. For most of the year, she had help in the house, but she'd sent the cook and the maids home for Christmas. Burnside Farm was prosperous, and Rhona had got used to having servants when she was in London.

How things had changed since she'd struggled to tend to her father back in their ramshackle cottage in the Highlands. Christmas in London had been a matter of giving orders to the housekeeper, overseeing decorations for the house, then playing hostess to the often riotous celebrations. These days, the holiday was much quieter, with just her son to share her festive table.

Except today for the first time, her family would be complete. Which made her wonder whether Malcolm was awake. Even if he wasn't, she should check the fire in his room. The storm might have blown out, but it was freezing outside.

She made more tea and carried a cup down the corridor, noticing the drop in temperature the moment she left her cozy kitchen. Carefully, she opened the bedroom door and padded into the darkened room.

The fire had burned down but provided light enough for her to see that Malcolm remained unmoving under the mountain of bedclothes. He didn't stir as she set down the tea and crossed to add some wood to the fire and stoke it up.

She should leave him to sleep, but she couldn't resist creeping closer to the bed. The tenderness that threatened to turn her good, practical brain to porridge surged. Last night, he'd been so weary. Too weary for a man still only in his mid-thirties.

The roaring fire meant she could see him in perfect detail. He looked so much like Patrick that her silly heart flipped over and powerful emotion closed her throat. She reached out to smooth the untidy dark hair back from his forehead. When his thick eyelashes flickered up to reveal fathomless black eyes, she lifted her hand.

Unalloyed pleasure glowed in the gaze that settled on her. A smile so sweet curved his lips, that her doubts melted away to gooey syrup. For this brief instant, he was once again the handsome, ardent boy who had held her heart.

"Good morning, Rhona," he said softly.

The rich velvet baritone of his voice played a sensual melody up and down her spine. He reached out his hand and without thinking, she took it. The sure grip reminded her that she trusted him again and that he'd never wronged her.

It also sent a shock of heat rippling along her arm and made her heart start to skip about like a spring lamb in the sun. "Good morning, Malcolm," she murmured and couldn't help smiling back.

Before she could question the wisdom of what she did, she fell to her knees and leaned forward to place her lips on his.

The kiss was fleeting, but the shock of it cracked through her like a gunshot. Lips tingling, pulse drumming in her ears and making her deaf to anything else, she pulled away.

For a long moment, she stared into heavy dark eyes, reading surprised pleasure there. His grasp on her hand tightened. He shifted up in the bed, and his other hand snaked out to catch the back of her head.

"Come here," Malcolm whispered. With a gentle ruthlessness she couldn't resist, he drew her up until his lips met hers.

CHAPTER NINE

Malcolm knew he wasn't dreaming. This was too good to be a dream. Most of his dreams since he'd lost Rhona had verged closer to nightmares. Horrid, haunting, terrifying fantasies of her lost or in pain or dying.

He shifted in the bed until he could slide his arms around her where she kneeled on the floor. She curved into his embrace and with dizzying swiftness, the kiss turned carnal. Her mouth opened and when his tongue slipped inside, she sucked on it with immediate eagerness. She tasted of cinnamon and butter and passion.

When she pulled away after far too short an interval, he bit back an agonized groan. He was already hard for her, and she must know how he burned. He'd burned for more than twenty years, most of that in frustration and misery.

He braced to hear her tell him that she wanted to stop, that kissing him was a mistake.

What came out of her mouth wasn't an outright rejection, at least. "Wait," she said in a choked voice.

Wait? He felt like he'd spent his whole bloody life waiting. As he let her go, he stifled another groan.

Rhona rose and for one brief, vile moment, Malcolm expected her to walk out and leave him. Life hadn't encouraged optimism. He pushed back until he sat up against the pillows, the quilts pulled to his waist. If Rhona caught a glimpse of how rampant he was, he feared that she'd run away screaming.

She unwrapped the shawl from her shoulders, then fumbled with the flannel nightdress. The billowing white garment was designed more for warmth than seduction, although he was powerfully seduced.

As he watched her, every drop of moisture dried from his mouth. Could this be? He didn't dare speak, for fear that he might make her change her mind.

With dazed eyes, he saw her tug the nightdress over her head and discard it on the wooden floor. When she stood naked before him, his breath stopped and his voice jammed in his closing throat.

Her skin was still as white as milk, and the fiery hair on her head matched the fiery triangle of curls below her flat belly. Her breasts were fuller than he remembered, and crowned with beaded rose-pink nipples he'd never forgotten.

As his eyes feasted on her, his blood pounded like a wild ocean. She was beautiful, rounder and softer than the girl she'd been. But how he loved the womanly shape of her. He wanted to stare at her until he filled his memory with every inch of her lovely form.

Her cheeks turned pink, as she stood trembling under his hungry gaze. It turned out that she still blushed.

"Move over," she said in a strangled voice.

As he cooperated, still trapped in stunned silence, she dived into the bed. He seized her in shaking hands and twisted her until she lay flat.

Startled green eyes flashed up to stare at him as he rose above her. Unable to resist, he lowered his head to kiss her again, teasing her soft, lush lips. She reached up to bury her hands in his hair and hold him still for a kiss of such incendiary passion, he feared he was about to dissolve into smoking ash.

He'd imagined if he got Rhona into bed, all their time apart would make the encounter awkward. Full of hesitations and uncertainty. But she met his ardor with heart-stopping generosity.

She pulled away, panting and flushed, and her hand slid down his body to fit itself to his throbbing hardness. As sizzling arousal shuddered through him, he groaned. He shifted to the side to give her better access and rose on one elbow so he could watch her expression.

He loved that she wasn't shy. This was a woman who met him without demur or doubt. Her mature passion was a heady wine indeed. When his cock swelled under her touch, a triumphant smile lifted her lips. He couldn't resist kissing her again, brief and hard, as she fiddled with the fastenings on his breeches.

When her hand closed around his naked length, he groaned again and angled his hips forward into her grip. He cupped her breast, and she gasped and tightened her hold, making stars explode behind his eyes. Dipping his head, he drew her nipple into his mouth. He teased it with his tongue until her breath emerged in sharp little huffs.

Malcolm was shaking, starving for her. After so long, he wanted to savor every second, draw out the pleasure, but the heat between them already rose to scorching levels. This would be no leisurely loving. He'd yearned for this union. Now he could brook no delay.

He moved over her and settled between her thighs. When she stared up at him, he caught a shadow in her beautiful eyes that made him pause.

"This doesn't mean anything, Malcolm." The edge in her voice contrasted with the soft ease of her body under his.

Since that first astounding kiss when he'd awoken to find her watching him with such tenderness, speech had deserted him. Now he found himself responding with a short laugh, full of affectionate amusement. "Of course it does, ye muddleheaded lassie. It means everything."

Before she could protest, he thrust forward and claimed her body. She cried out and dug her fingernails into his shoulders, and her eyes turned opaque with swift pleasure.

Malcolm lowered to press her deep into the soft mattress, and he buried his face in the curve of her shoulder. Her body offered him a hot welcome. She was sleek and tight and ready, despite the hurried preliminaries.

Since the day she'd left Dun Carron, the world had carved away his soul piece by piece. Rhona gave him back that soul. He felt like weeping. He felt like dancing. He felt like going on his knees to an Almighty he'd cursed too often over the years. Now, he wanted to beg forgiveness and offer up a profound gratitude.

He'd had no home for so long, but here, buried deep inside Rhona's body, he was home at last. Through his quaking pleasure, he felt her urgent grip on his shoulders relax into caresses.

She began to stroke him, long, exploratory touches across his taut shoulders and along his back and arms. Everywhere she touched, she lifted away another small chip of bitterness and left warmth and acceptance behind.

After a long time, he kissed her with all the love overflowing from his heart. Claiming Rhona all those years ago had been an act of joy and sunshine and hope. But the years of absence and sorrow and seeking lent tonight's union a significance that reached to the edges of eternity.

"Thank you," he said, his voice thick with emotion so powerful that it verged on pain.

When he raised his head, she looked stricken, even as she tightened around him with a breathtaking eagerness that made his heart crash against his ribs.

When he first joined his body with hers, he'd basked in the sublime stillness. But the urge to move was becoming irresistible. Still he clung as long as he could to this radiant connection.

She smoothed his hair away from his forehead, her hand trembling. "I'd...forgotten."

His lips lifted in a smile. "How it is between us?"

"I thought I must have imagined the way you make me feel like part of you, like you're part of me."

His smile intensified. "Och, you've always been part of me." Before she could argue or try to talk herself into dismissing this transcendent connection as a matter of mere physical release, he spoke. "Now let me show ye pleasure."

"Yes, please," she murmured and bucked up her hips with an enthusiasm that made his heart waltz with joy.

The change in position smashed through him like a blow. He closed his eyes and began to move, circling his hips until her moans told him he'd found her center of pleasure. He struggled to extend the delight, but he'd been too long without her and he wanted her too much. When he knew the inevitable moment approached, he lowered his hand to find the place between her legs that would send her over into ecstasy.

With a husky cry, she shook and clenched as rapture gripped her. His movements became wilder, before he released a guttural sigh and spilled into her womb in a gush of surrender.

Gasping, he slumped over her. He'd given her every drop of the man he was and the man he'd been. When he was a boy, she'd carved her name on his soul. The years since had only etched that possession more deeply. What they'd just done confirmed the truth that had dominated his life. He belonged to Rhona Macleod. Away from her, his life wasn't worth the air he breathed.

He wanted to stay crushed against her like this forever, but he must be squashing her. When he shifted, she caught his arms in frantic hands. "Not yet."

Her voice was laced with tears. Had what they'd just done touched her emotions as indelibly as it had touched his?

"That was glorious," he murmured.

"It was."

"I must be suffocating ye."

"I don't mind."

Appalled, he thought of something beyond the joy he'd just experienced. "Dear God, I forgot about Patrick. What will he think?"

At least that chased away her tears. Malcolm felt Rhona's low laugh through his entire body. They were still joined. "He's singing at St Margaret's all morning. He won't be back for a couple of hours yet."

Malcolm rolled off her and shifted higher against the pillows. "Come here."

He appreciated how willingly she wriggled up to curl into his side. Sliding an arm around her, he kissed her with all the weary joy that glowed in his heart.

She was warm and loose-limbed in his embrace. Lazy pleasure swirled in his blood as he recalled the unparalleled bliss of pumping into her.

He'd been so young the last time they'd lain together. The experience had been marvelous enough to set the pattern for the rest of his life. But in the blind fever of first love, he'd imagined that he could look forward to Rhona in his bed for years. His older self knew better than to take anything for granted.

"So you're mine for a little while longer yet."

She smiled without a trace of the wariness that had marked her dealings with him since he'd arrived yesterday afternoon. "At some stage, I need to check the animals and turn the goose in the oven."

"But no' now."

"No, not now." She laid her head on his chest and placed her hand flat on the heart that spoke her name with every beat.

How appropriate that Malcolm found his beloved at Christmas, the time of miracles. The sweetness of this quiet moment smoothed a balm over the wounds he'd suffered so long ago. He had his love in his arms, and for once, the world seemed to be on his side.

There was still so much he and Rhona had to work out, so much he needed to persuade her to accept. But he refused to think beyond this heavenly ease. Rhona was here. She'd given herself to him with a fervent passion that had humbled him, and she showed no inclination to leave.

This might be a temporary paradise, but after all his years in hell, he meant to linger in Eden as long as he could.

Malcolm didn't know how long he drifted in perfect contentment. He might have even dropped off into a fleeting doze. But at some stage, he became aware of Rhona's hand stroking his bare chest.

With a growl of approval, he opened his eyes. "What are ye doing to me?"

"Becoming reacquainted with the beauty sites I visited as a girl," she said.

He smiled, enchanted anew. It seemed the whimsical humor that had been such a charming characteristic of her younger self hadn't vanished altogether.

"Beauty sites? I'm a raddled old wreck these days."

She raised her face until she met his eyes, while that devilish disturbing stroking continued. Now she was touching his belly, with predictable results. He was surprised at the speed of his recovery. In that fiery consummation, he'd given her everything he had. He wouldn't have thought he retained such stamina.

Apparently love had its own magic. Love, and long abstinence.

"You were a beautiful boy, Malcolm. I used to look at you and go quite weak at the knees, even before I knew what you could do with your lips and hands and body." She leaned far enough away to conduct a thorough inspection of his chest. It turned out that her eyes could work their own magic.

It was a good thing Patrick was away. Malcolm started to weave some interesting ideas for how he and Rhona might occupy the next little while.

The smile that curved her voluptuous mouth, red after his kisses, expressed unashamed hunger. "You're still beautiful, despite a few extra lines and the odd bit of silver in your hair."

His lips quirked in wry disagreement. "The odd bit of silver? I'm almost as gray as Old Father Time."

"You must know you're still an attractive man, Malcolm."

He liked that she found him pleasing to look at. "As long as ye find me appealing, that's all that matters."

He was disappointed when a slight frown dimmed her smile. How he loved to see her smile. Every time she smiled at him, she set another star in the sky. His sky had been lifeless and dark too long.

"I can't be the only woman in all this time who has fallen under the spell of the brooding Laird of Dun Carron, who carries his secret sorrow like a badge of honor."

He shrugged. "I have nae idea. If you're asking if I've taken other lovers to my bed, the answer is no. I told you – I know what real love is. I wasn't going to accept a tawdry facsimile. And I pledged ye my faith. I'm a man of my word."

Horror darkened her gaze. To his regret, she stopped caressing him and sat up. "Oh, Malcolm, you can't have slept alone all these years."

His mouth tightened. "I can, and I have."

Moisture filled her eyes, and she cupped his jaw with a tenderness that sliced a jagged rift across his aching heart. "I'm so sorry I mistrusted you. I already knew you were remarkable when I loved you at Dun Carron. I had no idea how remarkable, though. Not a man in a million would keep true to a woman he thought was so long dead."

Her awestruck admiration made him uncomfortable, and he shifted against the rumpled sheets. "It's no' so remarkable. You spoiled me for other women, Rhona. After what we were to each other, how could I replace ye with an inadequate substitute?" He paused. "It wouldnae be fair on the substitute anyway."

Rhona stretched up and kissed him softly on the lips. During this last hour, they'd kissed often. Greedy, inflammatory kisses that fed their hunger for each other. This kiss spoke of sweetness and gratitude, perhaps even love. It cut deeper into his soul than the others.

This kiss told him that she'd never forgotten him either.

"I wasn't so faithful," she whispered. "I'm sorry."

Appalled, Malcolm pulled away to stare into tear-filled eyes. "Never apologize for marrying Samuel. I cannae deny that I was jealous at first. I still envy him the chance he had to see you blossom into this superb woman. I only saw the rose when she was a beautiful bud. Samuel saw ye flower into your full promise. But he kept you safe. He kept Patrick safe. If he hadn't, I would never have found you. I'd gladly live through the last eighteen years again, if I had the promise of finding ye at the end."

"Oh, Malcolm..." she said in a husky murmur and gave him another of those devastating kisses that spoke of the love that he knew she was still a long way from confessing in words. "I'm not worthy of you."

He smiled and spoke the truth that lived in his heart. "Of course you are, *mo chridhe*."

She shook her head. "You're deluded, but I won't argue if you're so determined to see me as a paragon."

He gave a brief laugh. He'd laughed more in these short hours with her than he had in years. Only now from the snug sanctuary of Rhona's bed did he realize quite how grim and joyless his years of searching had been. He hoped to Hades that this warmth was more than a temporary reprieve. It would be unbearable if he caught a whiff of hope for something better and fate ripped everything away from him again.

"Very wise."

She sobered. "But I wasn't talking about what I did with Samuel when I said I was unfaithful to you. There was a greater betrayal."

"That you didnae trust me enough to know I'd never scheme to send you away."

That had hurt. By heaven, that had felt like someone ripping out his guts with red-hot pincers.

"Yes." Guilt and regret weighted her peridot gaze. "I hope you can forgive me."

He frowned as he thought about what she said. "Of course I forgive you. You recognized the truth fast enough when I presented it to ye."

Relief eased her frown. She picked up his hand and brought it to her lips. More of that dangerous tenderness that had his heart turning somersaults. "I still should have kept faith."

She lowered his hand but kept hold of it. After what they'd just done, the contact should feel casual. Instead, it felt like she captured him in an eternal spell.

Except she'd already done that years ago, and he'd never tried to break free. He was content to be in her thrall.

She went on in a low voice. "But even when I cursed you for rejecting me, I still felt unfaithful every time Samuel used my body. So something inside me was always yours, no matter how often I told myself that I hated you."

He didn't mistake the magnitude of her admission. "Rhona..." he forced out and swept her into his arms for a kiss that spoke all the vows he wouldn't yet let himself say aloud.

They were both gasping when they drew apart, and her eyes were smoky with desire. He smiled with all the delight he took in her. "Will the goose wait?"

She smiled back. "Devil take the goose. When I've got a fine Scottish laddie in my bed, I've got better things to worry about than cooking."

Malcolm laughed with an unfettered joy he hadn't felt in too long. What a woman she was. He'd loved the bonny lass. He came to adore the strong, passionate woman the lass had turned into.

"Well, dinnae let me talk you out of that opinion." He dragged her down into the bed and began to explore the luscious curves he hadn't paid nearly enough attention to in the wild rush of their first encounter. Her soft murmurs of encouragement were the sweetest music he'd ever heard.

CHAPTER TEN

*I*t was late, after midnight, and Rhona was back in her favorite place in the house, the armchair in front of the kitchen fire. She was sipping fragrant mulled wine, the drink's warmth only mirroring the warmth glowing inside her.

It had been a marvelous Christmas, the best she'd ever known. Patrick had come back from his duties as a chorister in the early afternoon to discover his parents respectably dressed and conversing in obvious amity in the greenery-bedecked parlor. She hid a smile now as she recalled how she and Malcolm had scrambled to be clothed and ready. She'd hurried away to finish preparations for their meal, and Malcolm had looked after the animals without a word of complaint, so that Patrick would arrive back to a home in good order for Christmas dinner.

Malcolm's willingness to pitch in and help reminded her of something she'd always liked about the heir to Dun Carron. He had no airs and graces and didn't ever think that as the laird's son, he was above manual labor. That hadn't changed now he was the laird, she was pleased to see.

Actually it turned out that a lot of the things she'd liked about his younger self still appealed to her. He was kind, he was good-natured, and his sense of humor might be rusty with disuse, but he could still make her laugh.

Throughout lunch, her heart kept catching on special moments as Patrick and Malcolm eased their way into an understanding. It had been so moving to watch as the two most significant men in her life established what promised to become a strong rapport. At last, she let herself acknowledge how much her son owed to his father. The essential sweetness. The perceptiveness. The natural consideration for others.

Her thoughts turned, as was inevitable, to those sublime hours she and Malcolm had spent alone together this morning. It turned out that he could still summon responses that transformed the world to starlight. At the first touch of those thin, elegant hands, she'd melted into a puddle of desire, and she still quivered with a need she hadn't felt since she was a girl. A need stronger than she remembered, however heady their youthful passion had been.

Now she wanted Malcolm with a woman's desire and that proved to be a thousand times more heated than an inexperienced girl's craving. A flush rose in her cheeks as she remembered shuddering through each explosive climax.

The first time they came together, she'd imagined nothing could compare with the pleasure. Then Malcolm set out to please her again, using his hands and his mouth to fling her high into a fiery sky. The slow seduction culminated in a last joining that exploded all her previous experience of bliss into a conflagration that left her shaking and crying and feeling made anew.

It was lucky the Christmas dinner hadn't emerged from the oven as charred remains. The goose had been a little dry, but delicious for all that.

Now she closed her eyes and rested her head back on the chair as she relived that sizzling interval in Malcolm's arms. She'd forgotten the delights of a young, vigorous lover. Samuel had been tender and kind, but with him, she'd never scaled the heights of pleasure that she had with Malcolm at Dun Carron. She'd come to believe she never would again.

It turned out she was wrong about that. A morning in bed with Malcolm demonstrated that desire had merely been banked, not extinguished. One touch from the right man's hand, and the flames inside her had roared into an uncontrollable blaze.

Rhona wanted to do it all again. And soon. It turned out that the respectable widow wasn't so respectable after all.

"You're smiling," a soft baritone said.

She lifted heavy eyelids to see Malcolm standing in front of her, his back to the fire. He could move like a cat when he wanted to. Or perhaps she'd been too lost in steamy reminiscences to notice that she was no longer alone.

"Good evening," she murmured, her gaze eating him up with unabashed enjoyment.

He was dressed in the shirt and breeches he'd worn during the day, but he'd removed his neck cloth and dark blue coat. She caught a glimpse of his strong throat and the dusky curls on his chest. Curls that had provided stimulating friction under her palms when they'd lain naked together.

"Good evening to ye," he returned, black eyes devouring her as if she was a piece of the buttery shortbread they'd all made such pigs of themselves on at supper.

A fresh tide of arousal flowed through her, and she shifted on her chair as something inside her loosened and melted in longing. Heaven help her. Five years without a man, and now all she could think of was bed sport.

And Malcolm hadn't even touched her. One glance from those hot dark eyes, and she went up in smoke.

"Right now, I'm wishing Patrick to Hades, even if I love every hair on his handsome head," she admitted.

Malcolm gave a grunt of laughter. His smile was no longer a grim twist of his lips. He looked younger. If meeting him again had revived the willful girl she'd once been, he, too, bore a much closer resemblance to the dashing young lad she'd loved with such desperation.

"You're most welcome to come and lie in my arms again, the way we did last night."

She sent him a direct look. "Will that be enough for you?"

He shrugged. "Having rediscovered how it feels to make love to ye, no. But on the other hand, I dinnae want to be apart from you, and if that's the best we can manage, it's something."

Her heart performed a dizzying leap. He lowered all his defences against her. She wanted to warn him to be careful. He made it too clear that she wielded enormous power over him. She feared where they were heading. She feared hurting him, when he'd already suffered so much. But it was mad to think about forever. They'd only reunited a little over a day ago.

Her good sense insisted on self-protection, on retreating from this encroaching closeness.

Nonetheless, she found herself giving him a candid reply. "I don't want to be apart from you either, but I don't like my son knowing that I can't keep my hands off you."

"He's a clever boy." Malcolm's glance was mocking. "I suspect he may have already guessed."

Rhona sighed and set her half-empty mug on the small table near her chair. "You could be right."

"I dinnae want to make things difficult for you."

As if she believed that. His arrival made her life infinitely more complicated, and from what she could see, he had no qualms about that at all. She rose to her feet. "Would you like some mulled wine?"

He stepped closer, looming over her in a way that did nothing to bolster her self-control. Mixed with the fresh fragrance of Christmas greenery and the spices in the wine, she caught the drift of Malcolm's clean male scent. Desire tugged against common sense, and looked sure to win the battle.

"Aye, please. But first, there's something I must do."

Puzzled, she looked up at him. "Oh?"

"This." The devilish smile curving his lips warned her of his intentions. He didn't catch her unawares when he drew her into his arms for a leisurely kiss that left her staggering by the time he finished.

"Oh, my," she whispered, clinging to his shoulders so she didn't collapse into a heap at his feet.

He smiled and kissed her once more, before stepping away and leaning his hips against the bench. "How do ye think Patrick is coping with everything?"

Before she could answer, Rhona needed a few seconds to banish the haze that blanketed her brain after that kiss. "On the surface, he's taken it all in his stride. But it's been a day and a half of dramatic, life-changing revelations, and he'll need time to come to terms with what has happened. At least he likes you."

To her surprise, Christmas dinner had been lighthearted fun, but once they returned to the warmth of the kitchen in the afternoon, Malcolm and Rhona had at last told Patrick about the events leading up to his birth. He'd listened in uncharacteristic stillness, and she could see that the story left a deep impression on him. He remained more pensive than usual when he went to bed.

She wasn't surprised. It was a lot for a young man to take in. For anyone, really.

All three of them had sat talking until nearly eleven, and Rhona had the strangest feeling that the long, intense discussion had forged bonds that could never break.

The faint smile that lightened Malcolm's face turned him into the image of her son. At least after this Christmas, that resemblance would no longer set her heart cramping with agony.

"I like him, too." He ran his hand through his rumpled, silver-streaked hair and his voice deepened with emotion. "By God, I love him. I always knew I would, but that doesnae change the shock or the power of the feeling when it hit me. He's an impressive young man. I'm proud to call him my son. You did a wonderful job bringing him up."

She made a dismissive gesture. "I take no credit for that. Patrick was born good. You've never seen such a beautiful baby, and he never cried or caused trouble."

Rhona regretted that she'd spoken when sadness darkened Malcolm's eyes. "I'm sorry I didn't see that. I'm sorry I wasnae there to watch him grow up."

As pity made her eyes mist, she took his arm. "I wish I could make up for everything that you've missed."

It was startling how natural it felt to touch him. In fact, she'd reached a stage where it felt unnatural not to touch him. Goodness knew what state she'd be in if he stayed much longer. Already she fell back into the intimacy they'd once shared.

She struggled to remind herself that after all this time apart, Malcolm was a stranger. But he felt even less like a stranger than he had last night. And he hadn't felt much like a stranger then.

When he laid his hand over hers, warmth surged up her arm and settled in her troubled heart. "At least I've found ye both. And after today, Patrick knows about his heritage and his inheritance."

Rhona struggled to lighten the portentous atmosphere building between them. It had been a long day, crammed with emotional strain. She wasn't sure she was up to facing any more demands right now. She forced herself to smile, although she wouldn't wager a groat on how convincing it was. "He rather fancies himself as king of the castle."

To her relief, Malcolm responded with a short laugh. "Let's hope he still feels like that when he sees it."

They'd made no arrangements for a visit, but she assumed Malcolm wanted Patrick to come to Dun Carron as soon as possible. She suspected he'd want their son to live there, too, at least some of the time, so he could make a place for himself as the heir.

Rhona hoped to heaven the clan accepted him. His obvious resemblance to his father should help.

Today had been very much focused on the past. She had an inkling that tomorrow might mark the start of plans for the future.

Malcolm must have had a similar thought because he lifted her hand from his arm and drew her toward the center of the floor. "What about you, Rhona? Are ye going to come back to Dun Carron?"

Her heart did another of those disconcerting cartwheels. She tugged her hand free and buried it in her skirts to hide its shaking. She wasn't sure she was ready to have this conversation. "How can I? Everybody knows about the old scandal."

His dark eyes were somber and unwavering. "How can you no'? It's your home."

"It hasn't been my home since I was a silly girl, carrying your bastard in my belly."

He flinched. "Dinnae call Patrick that. In my mind, he's my legitimate son."

Old cynicism twisted her lips. "That's all well and good, but in everyone else's mind, I'm a slut and he's your by-blow. I have a good life and an unblemished reputation here in Muirburgh. Why should I give those up?"

Malcolm remained composed under her attack. She should be used to that by now. "You have a place at Dun Carron as my wife, Rhona. In my heart, you've always been my wife. If we make it official and ye become the glen's lady, who will care about what we did twenty years ago?"

She frowned, even as her asinine heart told her to throw herself into his arms and tell him she was happy to spend the rest of her life with him. "Malcolm, this isn't fair. You only turned up last night. It's too soon."

The stubbornness that had appeared so often since he'd arrived hardened his features. "I came here last night after a lifetime of loving ye. I still love ye. Nothing that has happened since then has changed that. The question now is how do you feel about me."

He still loved her. He told her so.

She'd been right to fear that emotional honesty. *I still love you.* Those four words contained such power. Her heart swelled with dangerous pleasure, even as fear prickled across her skin.

"I...I don't know," she said and cursed herself as a coward.

Because she had an inexorable suspicion that she loved him, too. She had a horrible feeling that she'd never stopped loving him.

When he growled his dissatisfaction with that answer, she couldn't blame him. "Ye can do better than that."

She bit her lip and spread her hands in bewilderment. "I want you."

"Aye."

She gulped for more breath to feed her starved lungs and battled to answer him in a way that kept her vulnerable heart safe. He was asking her to risk so much on what she'd felt as a girl. "I like you. A lot. I like how you are with Patrick. I'm overjoyed that you two are likely to grow closer. You're so similar."

He sliced the air with a decisive hand. "This isnae about Patrick. This is about you and me."

She backed away, shaking her head. Butterflies the size of elephants danced a jig in her stomach. "I'm afraid."

His expression softened. "I know you are."

Her lips flattened in annoyance. "So why are ye forcing this issue tonight?"

He sighed and once more, ran one hand through his hair, leaving it charmingly ruffled. "You're right. It's no' fair to push for a commitment so fast. I promised to court you, and I meant it." His voice was low and vibrating with intensity. "But that was before you came to my bed. That was before I spent Christmas with ye and my son. Everything has changed. Yet nothing has changed."

"Malcolm…" she stammered, both dreading and longing to hear what he said next.

His eyes burned into hers. "Rhona, my heart has never wavered from loving you. It never will. I hoped…I think ye might still love me, even if you're not ready to admit it. I'll woo you until doomsday if you want, but we've already lost so much time when we could have been happy together. Must we waste even more time, when you have to see that ye and I belong together? We always have."

She swallowed to ease a throat crammed with thorny emotion and told her heart to stop leaping about in her chest like a mad thing. "You…you're asking me to throw caution to the winds."

His smile was so full of unconditional love, she wanted to cry. "I am. Not to mention I dinnae want to spend the next few months sneaking around every time I want to hold you in my arms. We had quite enough of that back in the old days."

He had a point. After this morning, how could she settle for a chaste courtship? "I don't want that either," she admitted reluctantly.

His eyes locked on her with an implacable purpose that she felt to her bones. "Will you marry me, Rhona?"

She stared at him while the silence extended. And extended.

A sensible woman would say no, but the refusal wouldn't pass her lips. Instead, her mind winnowed their long and agonizing history. Love. Tragedy. Loneliness. And now, at last, perhaps a chance that they could mend all the rifts and step forward into life as man and wife.

"It would take so much courage," she murmured, her voice unsteady.

"You've never lacked courage, my darling." He extended his hand toward her. "I love ye. Do you love me?"

Tears rushed to her eyes and those butterflies collided hard in her stomach, but how could she lie? "Yes, plague take you, I love you."

She watched the strain of years ease from his face. "And will ye make a life with me?"

Ever since she'd been ripped so violently away from her home and everyone she loved – including, most of all, the man who stood before her now, asking her to make an impossible promise – she'd done her best to stay safe and to keep her son safe. Accepting Malcolm's proposal after all these years apart wasn't safe at all. But perhaps it was time to seek some adventure and trust that her heart knew best.

Trembling, she took his hand. "I think you and I are going back to Dun Carron."

His fingers curled around hers with a firmness that she knew would never fail her. She hadn't seen that glittering light in his eyes since their days at Dun Carron. "Is that yes?"

The tears overflowed as she stepped closer on shaky legs. The truth, long-hidden but always present, surged up to find voice. "Yes, Malcolm. I'm yours. I've always been yours."

"Och, my beloved, that was worth waiting almost twenty years to hear," he whispered and drew her into his arms for a kiss of invincible love.

EPILOGUE

Dun Carron Castle, Western Highlands of Scotland, Christmas 1834

"I wish Patrick Ashley-Innes, my beloved son, and his bonny wife-to-be, Sheena Balfour, many joyful years together. May Patrick and his lovely bride be as happy as I've been with my sweet and biddable Rhona."

From where he stood halfway up the staircase, Malcolm heard a general rumble of mirth from the people crowded into the castle's cavernous great hall to celebrate both the festive season and Patrick's engagement to the daughter of a neighboring landowner.

Over the last ten years, Christmas at Dun Carron had turned into a lively, cheerful occasion, not least because the laird and his family always made sure they joined their kinfolk for the holiday. This year with the announcement of Patrick's forthcoming marriage, the day was doubly bright.

Malcolm tightened his grip on Rhona's still-slender waist and glanced down into her glowing eyes. She'd brought laughter back to the castle from the moment she'd returned as his wife, a few days after he'd found her that snowy evening in Muirburgh.

On that long ago night, he'd been sure that he couldn't love her more than he did. He was wrong. A decade of marriage had strengthened the bond between them, forged in youthful passion, tested through lies, separation, and grief, only to emerge stronger and surer than ever at the last.

"It's a fortunate fellow who is possessed of an obedient wife, my darling," she said, the voice that had once enthralled the theatergoers of London effortlessly rising above the hubbub.

Her impudent reply sparked another fond laugh from their guests. While Malcolm might tease her about her dauntlessness, he was delighted that his wife was brave enough to stand up for what she believed was right for her family and her people. His soul had always recognized her as a true equal. He had reason to be grateful for that courage and spirit. Without it, she'd never have survived to come back to him.

Rhona had returned to the glen to make her mark as his genuine partner, and while a few people remembered the old shame and scandal, Malcolm had made it very clear that an insult to the lady of Dun Carron was an insult to the laird. In truth, the clan had accepted Rhona as chatelaine and Patrick as heir more easily than he'd expected. The old Highland tradition of handfasting, where a couple married by making their vows before witnesses, meant that in many minds, Malcolm and Rhona were wed before her banishment from the estate.

"Och, how would the Innes ken anything about an obedient wife, my lady?" Old Billy McIntyre called out from below. "He didnae pick a lily-livered Sassenach, but a fiery Scots lass to keep him warm."

Malcolm laughed. "Aye, that's true, Billy. Rather, I'll say fortunate is the laddie who married Rhona Innes and brought her back to where she belongs."

A murmur of approval greeted that statement, as Rhona's expression softened with the love that illuminated every minute of Malcolm's life. "I belong with you, my dear husband," she said, her words meant for his ears only. "I thank the Good Lord every day that you found me all those Christmases ago."

Because Christmas wasn't just a time for the clan to come together. It also marked the anniversary of the date when his life, that had gone so tragically wrong, took an abrupt turn in the right direction.

Malcolm bent to give her a quick kiss, feeling her lips soften under his. He felt giddy when she drew away, too soon in his opinion. Although he and his gorgeous wife had planned their own private celebration later, in the laird's opulent suite of rooms in the south tower.

"So do I, *mo chridhe*, so do I," he murmured and smiled into the flashing green eyes that had stolen his heart when he was a boy. A sideways glance from those eyes still made his legs wobble and his heart perform acrobatics, even all these years later.

The passing of time had hardly marked Rhona. As he looked at her in her stylish sapphire blue silk gown – her penchant for bright colours persisted, he was pleased to say – she remained the unforgettable lassie he'd fallen in love with. There might be a few more laugh lines, but the contentment in her expression would keep her lovely until her dying day.

He on the other hand was as silvery white as any mountain hare hopping across Ben Nevis. Rhona said she didn't mind, and he had to believe her. When she looked at him, she looked with the eyes of steadfast love, so he supposed a few gray hairs didn't matter much.

But tonight wasn't about him and the woman he loved. Or at least not yet. It was about the fine young man they'd created together in a sunlit summer dell at Dun Carron twenty-eight years ago. Malcolm raised his glass of champagne toward Patrick and exquisite, golden-haired Sheena. The young couple stood a step above, holding hands and looking dazzled with happiness.

"My kinfolk, my family, my friends, I ask ye all to wish the very best to the exceptional young man who has always made me Scotland's proudest father and to the splendid lass who has won his heart."

"To Patrick and Sheena," Rhona said beside him, raising her glass, too. "May you both enjoy the same abiding love that has sustained Malcolm and me."

Through the tide of congratulatory goodwill that ensued, Malcolm drew his wife close against his side and turned to her with a smile. He clinked his glass with hers. "And here's to ye, my one and forever love."

Tears misted those peridot eyes as she whispered in return, "And to you, the man I've always loved and I will always love. Here's to a lifetime of Christmases together. I'll never forget the night that you came back to me and made my life complete."

Lost for words, moved, adoring, Malcolm leaned down and kissed his wife with lingering delight as their audience cheered to the rafters.

ABOUT THE AUTHOR

Australian Anna Campbell has written 11 multi award-winning historical romances for Avon HarperCollins and Grand Central Publishing. As an independently published author, she's released more than 30 bestselling stories. Right now, she is working on a new series called A Scandal in Mayfair, set amidst the glamour and sensuality of Regency London. Anna has won numerous awards for her stories, including RT Book Reviews Reviewers Choice, the Booksellers Best, the Golden Quill (three times), the Heart of Excellence (twice), the Write Touch, the Aspen Gold (twice), and the Australian Romance Readers' favorite historical romance (five times).

Anna loves to hear from her readers. You can find her at:

Website: www.annacampbell.com

facebook.com/AnnaCampbellFans

twitter.comAnnaCampbellOz

bookbub.com/authors/anna-campbell

The Laird's Willful Lass:
The Lairds Most Likely Book 1

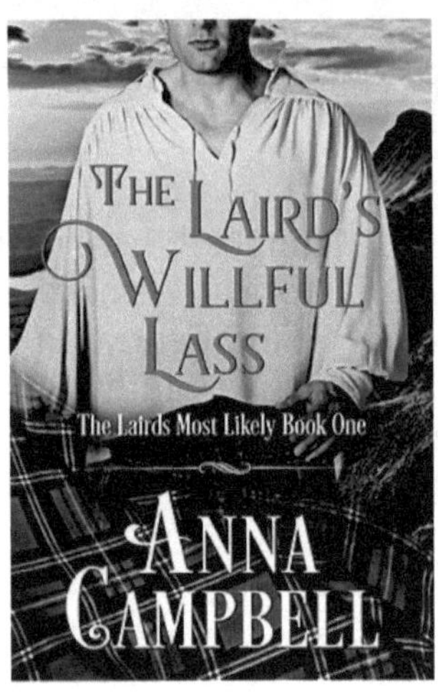

An untamed man as immovable as a Highland mountain...

Fergus Mackinnon, autocratic Laird of Achnasheen, likes to be in charge. When he was little more than a lad, he became master of his Scottish estate, and he's learned to rely on his unfailing judgment. So has everyone else in his corner of the world. He sees no reason for his bride—when he finds her—to be any different.

A headstrong woman from the warm and passionate south...

Marina Lucchetti knows all about fighting her way through a wall of masculine arrogance. In her native Florence, she's become a successful artist, no easy feat for a woman. Now a commission to paint a series of Highland scenes promises to spread her fame far and wide. When a carriage accident strands her at Achnasheen for a few weeks, it's a mixed blessing. The magnificent landscape offers everything her artistic soul could desire. If only she can resist the impulse to smash her easel across the laird's obstinate head.

When two fiery souls come together, a conflagration flares.

Marina is Fergus's worst nightmare—a woman who defies a man's guidance. Fergus challenges everything Marina believes about a woman's right to choose her path. No two people could be less suited. But when irresistible passion enters the equation, good sense soon jumps into the loch.

Will the desire between Fergus and Marina blaze hot, then fade to ashes? Or will the imperious laird and his willful lass discover that their differences aren't insurmountable after all, but the spice that will flavor a lifetime of happiness?

The Laird's Christmas Kiss:
The Lairds Most Likely Book 2

Down with love!

Ever since she was fifteen, shy wallflower Elspeth Douglas has pined in vain for the attentions of dashing Brody Girvan, Laird of Invermackie. But the rakish Highlander doesn't even know she's alive. Now she's twenty, she realizes that she'll never be happy until she stops loving her brother's handsome friend. When family and friends gather at Achnasheen Castle for Christmas, she intends to show the world that she's all grown up, and grown out of silly crushes on gorgeous Scotsmen. So take that, my gallant laddie!

Girls just want to have fun...

Except it turns out that Brody isn't singing from the same Christmas carol sheet. Elspeth decides she's

not interested in him anymore, just as he decides
he's very interested indeed. In fact, now he looks
more closely, his friend Hamish's sister is pretty
and funny and forthright – and just the lassie to
share his Highland estate. Convincing his little
wren of his romantic intentions is difficult enough,
even before she undergoes a makeover and
becomes the belle of Achnasheen. For once in his
life, dissolute Brody is burdened with honorable
intentions, while the lady he pursues is set on
flirtation with no strings attached.

Deck the halls with mistletoe!

With interfering friends and a crate of imported
mistletoe thrown into the mix, the stage is set for a
house party rife with secrets, clandestine kisses,
misunderstandings, heartache, scandal, and love
triumphant.

The Highlander's Lost Lady:
The Lairds Most Likely Book 3

A Highlander as brave and strong as a knight of old...

When Diarmid Mactavish, Laird of Invertavey, discovers a mysterious woman washed up on his land after a wild storm, he takes her in and tries to find her family. But even as forbidden dreams of sensual fulfillment torment him, he's convinced that this beautiful lassie isn't what she seems. And if there's one thing Diarmid despises, it's a liar.

A mother willing to do anything to save her daughter...

Widow Fiona Grant has risked everything to break free of her clan and rescue her adolescent daughter from a forced marriage. But before her quest has barely begun, disaster strikes. She escapes her brutish kinsmen, only to be shipwrecked on Mactavish territory where she falls into her enemies' hands. For centuries, a murderous feud has raged between the Mactavishes and the Grants, so how can she trust her darkly handsome host?

Now a twisted Highland road leads to danger and passion...and irresistible love. But is love strong enough to banish the past's long shadows and offer these wary allies all that their hearts desire?

The Highlander's Defiant Captive:
The Lairds Most Likely Book 4

Peace in the glens means war in the bedchamber!

Scotland. 1699. In a time of heroes, the greatest hero of all is Callum Mackinnon, Laird of Achnasheen. Brave, reckless, canny, and handsome enough to turn any lassie weak at the knees, Callum is a legend in the wild corner of the Highlands where he rules. Now the young laird is determined to choose a new path for his clan and end the violent feud with the Drummonds, a conflict that has painted the glens red with blood for centuries. This means taking Bonny Mhairi Drummond, the Rose of Bruard, as his wife. When negotiations with her pig-headed father break down, Callum seizes matters into his own hands and kidnaps the fairest maiden in Scotland, swearing to make her his own.

Bonny Mhairi is the adored only child of Clan

Drummond's doughty chieftain and she's inherited all her father's courage and stubbornness. Not to mention his undying hatred for anyone called Mackinnon. When the Mackinnon chieftain steals her away from her home and vows to woo her into accepting him as her husband, she swears that she'll never consent to be his bride. But trapped inside her foe's castle, Mhairi finds it hard to cling to old certainties. She detests her arrogant jailer, even as he sparks a fierce, forbidden hunger in her soul.

Loving the enemy…

As Callum and Mhairi wage their passionate war of hearts, danger, treachery and desire circle closer and closer. When her father's army masses at the gates of Achnasheen, will Mhairi prove herself a Drummond now and forever? Or will new allegiances trump ancient hatred, as the desperate laird battles to win the lass he loves more than his life?

The Highlander's Christmas Quest: The Lairds Most Likely Book 5

She's found the man for her, but he has no plans to stay on her island. Perhaps it's time to try a little sabotage!

Scotland. 1725. The moment she sees handsome Dougal Drummond, Kirsty Macbain tumbles headlong into love. A chance storm a few days before Christmas has blown the gallant Highlander off-course to her father's isle of Askaval, but once he's repaired his boat, Dougal is determined to continue on his way. His bright blue eyes are firmly fixed on valiant deeds and a distant horizon. What does he care for a smart-mouthed, independent lassie who forms no part of his plans for his future?

Kirsty is convinced that if only she can keep Dougal on Askaval, he'll see how perfect they are together. With his boat out of action, he's trapped in her company. Some surreptitious midnight destruction

with a drill and a hammer might help true love to
win out. On the other hand, if Dougal discovers
what she's been up to, there will be the devil to pay.

Will this madcap Christmas deliver Kirsty's heart's
desire – or will her scheming see Dougal sailing
away to a life without her?

The Highlander's English Bride: The Lairds Most Likely Book 6

An impossible pairing...

Hamish Douglas, the mercurial Laird of Glen Lyon, has never got along with independent, smart-mouthed Emily Baylor. Which wouldn't matter if this brilliant Scottish astronomer didn't move in the same scientific circles as Emily and if her famous father wasn't his mentor. But when Emily looks likely to derail the event which will make Hamish's career, he loses his temper with the pretty miss and his recklessness leaves her reputation in ruins.

A marriage made in scandal...

Emily has always thought her father's spectacular protégé was far too arrogant for his own good. But what is she to do when the only way she can save her good name in society is to wed the unruly laird? Reluctantly she accepts Hamish's proposal, but

only on the condition that their union remains
chaste. That shouldn't be a problem; they've never
been friends, let alone potential lovers – except that
after they marry, Hamish reveals unexpected
depths and a host of admirable qualities, and he's
so awfully handsome, and now the swaggering
rogue admits that he desires her...

***From the ballrooms of London to the
grandeur of the western Highlands, a battle
royal rages between these two strong-
willed combatants. Neither plans to yield
an inch – but are these smart people smart
enough to see that sometimes the greatest
victory lies in mutual surrender?***

The Highlander's Forbidden Mistress: The Lairds Most Likely Book 7

A week to be wicked…

Widowed Selina Martin faces another marriage founded on duty, not love. When notorious libertine Lord Bruard invites her to his isolated hunting lodge, he promises discretion – and seven days of hedonistic pleasure before she weds her boorish fiancé. All her life, Selina has done the right thing, but this no-strings-attached chance to discover the handsome rake's sensual secrets is irresistible. She'll surrender to her wicked fantasies, seize some brief happiness, then knuckle down to a loveless union. What could possibly go wrong?

In a lifetime of seduction, Brock Drummond, the dashing Earl of Bruard, has never wanted a woman the way he wants demure widow Selina Martin. When Selina agrees to become his temporary lover, he soon falls captive to an enchantment unlike any other. He sets out to slake his white hot desire until only ashes remain, but as each day of forbidden delight passes, the idea of saying goodbye to his ardent mistress becomes more and more unbearable.

When scandal explodes around them and threatens to destroy Selina, Brock is the only person she can turn to. After so short a time, can she trust a man whose name is a byword for depravity?

Will this sizzling liaison prove a mere affair to remember? Or will their week of passion spark a lifetime of happiness for the widow and her dissolute Scottish earl?

The Highlander's Christmas Countess: The Lairds Most Likely Book 8

The new stableboy has a secret!

Kit Laing is a genius with Glen Lyon's horses and a favorite with his employer's family, but he isn't all he seems. In fact, the shy stablehand isn't a he at all. Kit is actually Christabel Urquhart, Countess of Appin, on the run from a greedy, violent stepbrother with designs on her fortune.

And the laird's handsome nephew has worked out just what it is.

Quentin MacNab, the dashing heir to Cannich, has had his suspicions about the new stable lad from the first. Kit is far too pretty to be a boy – and far too well spoken to be a servant.

Now passion and danger combine to create a Yuletide like no other.

When a snowstorm traps Kit and Quentin overnight in an isolated hut, the discovery of her true identity sparks a rushed marriage to stave off a scandal. But can the Christmas Countess learn to trust her charming new husband's promises of protection? Or will their fragile alliance fall victim to the evil forces assailing her?

The Highlander's Rescued Maiden: The Lairds Most Likely Book 9

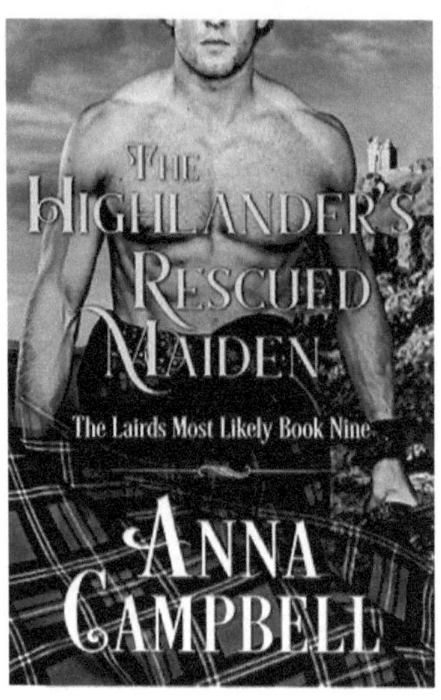

The myth of Fair Ellen of the Isles.

Across the Highlands, people recount the legend of a beautiful lassie in a tower, locked away from her clamorous suitors by a tyrannical father. Any person of sense dismisses the story as a fairy tale, no more substantial than a wisp of Scottish mist.

Rogue or hero? Or a little bit of both?

Dashing Highlander Will Mackinnon is a devil with the ladies, disinclined to fall for such romantic nonsense. But one day, his storm-tossed boat washes ashore at a rocky island dominated by a stone tower. Inside the tower, he discovers lovely, gallant Ellen Cameron and a passion that eclipses anything he's experienced before in his reckless life.

Danger and desire...

This brave adventurer vows to rescue the captive maiden and make her his own forever. But dark shadows gather about the lovers and threaten to destroy all their hopes for happiness. Will has found the love of a lifetime – but will it end up costing him his life?

The Highlander's Christmas Lassie: The Lairds Most Likely Book 10

Young love torn apart.

As teenagers, Malcolm Innes and Rhona Macleod fell passionately in love. But Malcom's parents were horrified to think of the aristocratic heir to Dun Carron marrying a humble crofter's daughter. Desperate to crush the affair, they locked Malcolm up and exiled Rhona to London where she disappears. But Malcolm is faithful and stubborn and devotes his life to searching for his beloved and the child she was carrying when they were cruelly separated.

A chance to mend two shattered lives.

On a snowy Christmas Eve, Rhona opens the door of her isolated farmhouse to find the man she never thought to see again, the man who betrayed her. When she was pregnant with his son, Malcolm abandoned her to find her way alone in a cold, heartless world. Now she discovers that her long-held hatred is based on lies and that he's been true to her. Yet surely after all these years, it's too late to awaken the love that once united them.

As Christmas Eve turns into Christmas Day, Malcolm and Rhona discover that their mutual desire has never died. Will this Yuletide reunion lead to a lifetime together? Or has old tragedy ruptured their bond forever?

9 781925 980189